FOREST LIFE

FOREST LIFE
Copyright {c} 2012 by Shane Crash
ISBN # 978-0615684246
Published by Civitas Press, LLC
San Jose, CA
www.civitaspress.com

Shane Crash
www.shanecrash.com/
twitter.com/shanecrash

Printed in the United States of America

FOREST

LIFE

BY
SHANE CRASH

CivitasPress
Publishing inspiring and redemptive ideas.[sm]

This book is for those who choose compassion in a cynical world: for my wife, my teachers, my family and all the memories that slip through the cracks.

CONTENTS

CHAPTER 1

This is a nice place to die.

Last night I dreamt of all the things I've lost. I'm awake now, but my mind is still shut up in a house I've built out of her bones. Her memory. I'm a half-thing, a semblance of someone who was once alive and whole. Walking through flowering rhododendrons toward the shores of Kentucky Lake, black walnuts and red poppies in my wake.

Is there such a thing as infallible love? If a man loses his wife and in an act of grief takes a straight razor from his elbow to his wrist, is that infallible love? I don't know. I don't know if a person is meant to recover when love leaves. I've come out here to hide. I've come to hide because I cannot understand life. Explanations based on magic and invisible super beings do not satisfy me.

It's become increasingly difficult to continue living without answers. All the distractions I once relied upon to avoid these imponderables are gone. So here I sit in Paris, Tennessee, asking these questions at last. I've resolved to find answers before I end my life.

"This is a nice place to die," I whisper to no one.

I don't feel strange talking to myself. I only ever talk to myself. Lenai can't hear me. I know this is the truth; I think so anyway. Sometimes I believe I feel her move inside me. I feel her respond to my pitiful drivel. I tell myself that it is psychosomatic nonsense, but then I weep. How I long for those moments when I feel her entirely. In those moments it doesn't matter whether it's real or make-believe. My love is near.

There is no chance I'll live to see the other side of this year. The forests here in Paris are blossoming and flowering, and I'm an old dead tree. Each night at dusk I sit amongst the poppies with this blade in hand, intending to cut. Straight razors are out of fashion, but I imagine they will always be romanticized in regards to suicide. I found this old beauty with a French point while pillaging my grandfather's house after his death.

I place the razor back into its sheath. I'm not going to cut today. I'm going to sober up and remember a while longer, at least until I'm strong enough to bid the world farewell.

It's easy to look back and see when my mind began to fray and wear out. It began with Lenai's death. It's all so clear in this quiet place. My mother died from a ruptured appendix and infected kidney when I was three. That's all I know about her for the most part. I never knew my father. My grandpa never made a fuss about raising me, and I never made a fuss about not knowing the man who conceived me. His death was the first time I'd ever experienced love leaving. It was then I decided that life is what it is and it has always been full of unanswered questions.

My grandpa was a good man. He was steady and stern, not controlled by his emotions. He was not an emotionally immature person, and he passed that on to me.

"God bless the man who can stay a man," he would say to me. "God bless the man who takes a stand."

The past has left its prints on everything, but that doesn't mean I'm any closer to achieving any understanding about it. I've run out of distractions and although my drunkenness blurs my thoughts, it also amplifies my despair.

The night is a terrible swelling. Its darkness, silence and solitude weigh on me each night. Since the accident I've tried to maintain contact with what was, but it is easier to feel close to the past on this dark porch just above the waterline. When I'm not careful the warm air and cicada songs can break me out of my illusion into some small forgetfulness. When this happens I dimly feel a twinge of despair in the back of my brain and return guilt ridden to my suffering. The truth is that all my self-reflection ends in saline-coated imponderables. It's all I can do to concede defeat and just plaster my brains on the wall. I'm resigned to the truth that I'll likely never find a home again, in my mind or elsewhere.

My poverty has a sort of sweetness about it. At times I feel as though I'm able to latch on and consciously milk it. It takes no effort on my part to move about the woods of Tennessee like a ghost. Mostly I stick to the outskirts of the lake next to my cabin. I get drunk and stumble around. I study the trees and smell the moss and sap. There are some beautiful flowering dogwoods across from where I sit now. They smell like hell.

I've been here nearly a month and, apart from my landlord's infrequent visits, I've been completely ignored. Mr. Locke, my landlord, is a solid human being as far as I can tell. His persona counters his appearance. He is a gentle spirit imprisoned in a calloused, worn-out shell of a body, always garbed in overalls and flannel. He was happy to rent out his lakefront cabin to me. After paying my deposit he made sure to let me know he'd keep me in his prayers as I *searched my soul*.

His simple statement was the catalyst for the thinking I did in those next days, trying to decide if a soul was a real thing. Although I haven't been able to form a definitive opinion about the reality of souls, last night I decided both that consciousness meant something, and that something feels fractured within me. I don't know how to feel. I don't know if what is broken inside of me can be put back together. Is whatever it is that is fractured my "soul?"

The nihilist in me is at once terrified and baffled that a force exists powerful enough to strip away the impenetrable walls of self-preservation. My faith may have withered but something amidst my despair whispers to me, urging me to hold on a little longer and endure. I know that something isn't Lenai, as often as I feel her permeate my mind and recollection. It's her void, her amputation that both presses the razor to my vein and removes it.

No, that something much larger and eternal that is fermenting amidst my aimless stumbling is something besides Lenai. It's become apparent to me that even if I should recover and not succumb to suicide, I'll inevitably have to lose my life, since life as I know it right now is not sustainable. Even if I continue living, whoever I was or am will cease to exist. I can't help but laugh to myself as I remember my grandfather's explanation of the phoenix metaphor.

"Everyone who lives and loves is a phoenix," he would say to me behind his pipe, his face lit up as if a phoenix dwelled within.

I still don't buy it and I likely never will. I don't think people recover from the loss of love. Everyone I love is dead. They're not here to answer my unanswerable queries. They can't tell me if they became a phoenix. Then there is the very physical reality that my being alone means there is no one around to help me stumble into bed when the American Honey culminates into unconsciousness. There is no one to hear my feet drag the wood floor. No one is watching for me as I inch toward the cabin doorway, drunk and stupid and fearful. No one will be affected by whether I cut myself, or not.

I lie here in this cabin, a ruined drunkard. The voices in my head sing out, painting a mural of how lost I've become, the last of my kind. The endless self-deprecation disgusts me as I stare out the bedroom window, admiring the hop hornbeams and black willows amidst the spruce paradise. They stare back at me, silently observing grief incarnate. I despise the way I see myself. I hate the silly way I romanticize my suffering to temper the sting. The truth is I'm alone and I no longer want to live.

The smell of the worn white pine flares my nostrils as I wrap my flannel blanket around my bones and take my usual spot on the floor. I don't sleep in the bed. It's an inviting queen-size utopia. It feels like a tribe of sirens, the worst sort of memory-inducing purgatory imaginable. I loathe the way it makes me remember the way such a bed used to feel.

I drift into dreams of Lenai and me, powerless against the dreamy recollections of the past. Three days prior to our departure from Ft. Lauderdale, I proposed. Two days prior to our departure from Ft. Lauderdale we made love. One day prior to our departure from Ft. Lauderdale I sold most of what I owned and purchased plane tickets. Two hours later we were on our way to the Caribbean.

We never stopped laughing from New York to Florida to Nassau.

She took me downtown and we spent hours sifting through Junkanoo handicrafts. We rode the Jitney Buses to Cable Beach and Paradise Island. We spent hours diving for conch shells and a fisherman taught us to cook them from his boat. These were the moments I first felt the nagging, something beyond the temporal. This was when I first felt the familiar fear. Fear that this heaven of loving and being loved by Lenai meant that losing it would be hell. I would lose the love holding me together. But there in Nassau, I was able to focus on Lenai and fight off the fear. She is what I required in that moment.

We drank too much at Senor Frog's and found ourselves aimlessly perusing the straw market. I emerged from the tents with braids in my hair and a thatched purse, realizing that I was completely powerless to the whims of my bride-to-be. Our love for each over spilled into everything we saw, and everyone we met, making every sight and encounter almost magical.

All of the locals were poor and their families were large. Everyone was kind and happy. When we returned to our hotel we examined the simplicity of it all. We marveled at the ambiguity between wealth and misery and poverty and contentment. We fell in love with the people. We made friends with a man named Josef and his eight children. They became our teachers. Josef's English took some getting used to; it was a strange mixture of Queen's diction, African influences and island lingo.

Regardless of the cultural barrier we became dear friends. We vowed to return, having fallen in love with not just the island, but also Josef's family.

"You're our family now," he told us, tears in his eyes, as we bid him farewell.

On our final evening we lay in bed, skin to skin, retiring into sheets warm and clean. Innumerable songs filled the air outside the hotel. Lenai's olive skin glowed ablaze beneath the white satin sheets. My fingertips climbed the ladder of her spine. I found forgetfulness in her myrtle green eyes. She was my bride-to-be, my life entire.

"Emmett," she smiled at me. The sound of my name on her lips rendered me mute so I responded by raising my eyebrows inquisitively. "It's all so senseless, isn't it?" She asked running her fingers over my forehead.

"What is, my love?" I feigned ignorance; though I was well aware that her father's recent death was on her mind.

"We live like everything ends at death. Do you think everything ends at death?" she whispered.

"I don't know darling. I just want to live entirely with you, right now." I pushed death from my mind, subconsciously afraid to think of life without her. She smiled in response, restoring peace to our world.

"Emmett, I need that too. But what if I can't live without knowing why I'm here?"

I could see that she wasn't content with my answer. "I don't know what to think," I muttered nervously. "People have been trying to figure that out since the beginning of time. All I know is that if there is an afterlife … I want to spend it with you."

Lenai's nose and forehead were pressed against mine. We were laughing and crying. We were hopeful. And so it went.

We loved with all we had in us, wrapped in sheets, feeling safe and whole.

We mirrored each other's thoughts and devised a solution. We railed and railed against senseless existence and vowed to lead a contemplative, disciplined life together. We began searching, and as we did, I began to feel less and less alone in my thoughts. We kissed on street corners and danced through the night.

Bright yesterdays and dark tomorrows,

The love and hate of the waking world.

I am awake. The dreams render me a trembling shell. There is nothing left of the hopeful lovers. Lenai is dead, she is buried in the ground, and I am a charred ruin incarnate, a collapsed steeple. In my mind I hear the soft lament of a phantom pressing keys on a piano.

I make my way to the living room and sit down in front of an old tarnished piano. It's smaller than a normal instrument of its kind. It was here when I moved in and I've mostly just ignored it. I tap on the keys and sip on a beer. I can't play but I try to sound out the imagined melody in my mind. Every hammer hit is dissonant and out of tune so I stop and rest my head above the keys.

I'm reluctant to sleep now, and I'm sober. These memories are like a disease. My sleeplessness leads me to the porch where I sit and listen to the soft wind dancing on the shore; the air and the grass have grown frosty. The sky grows gray in the twilight.

Nights like these cause a black loneliness. The shadows of the trees sweep over me and I swear some elemental force is attempting to comfort me. It is then that that "something," some imperceptible piece of my brain considers putting itself back together, but I try to resist it.

Lightning illuminates the dark landscape in front of me and I take note that the air has grown warmer. The thunder that follows is quick and booming, making me tremble, and the downpour begins shortly after. Heavy storms in such a small house stir claustrophobia and I'm relieved to see the world lit up from the shelter of the open porch.

I feel it all, the roaring undercurrent of uncertainty, and I am pained deeply by my doubt. It's the familiar doubt I feel about the last words my grandfather spoke to me.

"Try to love Emmett. Everything depends on it."

Sitting next to his bed, his words meant everything to me. Now, like all wisdom handed out to me, I find it trickling into naïve sentimentality. Does everyone find a truth? Is there a truth that never changes? Is there any worthwhile thing that death does not wither into nothingness? Is there a peace that surpasses understanding?

Whatever it was that once sustained my hope, or my forgetfulness, has gone away, destroyed by death. I cannot get it back, and I can't for the life of me stop thinking of suicide. I can't just end myself. This is a beautiful place to die. I couldn't ask for more. This place completely contrasts the dead forest within me, blacker than black. A forest all burned up.

My memories drift through my mind like soot and ash.

Lenai and I met while I was living in Green Point. Nearly every night I'd walk the streets while the neighborhood slept. I liked walking through Green Point at night; no one was out and it was almost silent. It was my way of escaping society without fleeing the city. I'd walk around and think about life, smoke a cigarette and plan for the future.

On April first I was walking like I normally do, enjoying the returning warmth of spring when I turned a corner and collided with Lenai. It seemed like fate to me. We were both horrified but we laughed it off. I apologized and continued on my walk. Two days later we ran into each other once more at the Brooklyn library. She sat at a table across from mine. It took her a few moments to notice me staring at her.

It seemed as though introductions were unnecessary. In a certain manner, it was as though we'd known each other long ago and stumbled back to one another. Wouldn't that make for a nice afterlife?

"That's one my favorites," she said, motioning toward the copy of *Slaughterhouse-Five* sitting next to me.

I had met many "Vonnegut fans" in my lifetime but few had ever been able to carry on a conversation with me regarding his work. It had become rather trendy to "like" that silly old man, but not so trendy to talk about his brilliant ideas. But that's exactly what I found myself doing that afternoon in the Brooklyn Library with a gorgeous stranger.

She had the intellectual capacity of a goddess. She was my better in so many ways. In those early days, sitting and discussing Kierkegaard and Tolstoy, her thoughts were stunning in both their complexity and simplicity. She'd laugh as I rambled on and on about comic books and my favorite band, The Mountain Goats, but then memorize the lyrics of my favorite songs.

"And I dreamt ... of a factory where they manufactured what I needed," she'd sing to me as I dozed off, lying next to her on the floor of my small flat. Sleep came so easy in those early days. We would walk through the snow. We'd talk for hours as we rode the subway, exploring the endless city. We were both expatriates to the Big Apple. We were hopeful college kids, aspiring for greatness.

In hindsight I mark the end of the easy, early days with the death of Lenai's father. His death nearly crippled her. I'll never forget the way in which his death shook her out of the ease of naïve unconsciousness

"What if something happens and you're taken from me, my love?" she asked me, her voice terrified, as we strolled through Brooklyn Park, her clutching my arm tightly. The fear stemming from her father's death threatened to spread through her, though it was never enough to drive us apart.

"I'll never leave you, Lenai." Those words became my modus operandi in response to her fear.

If only I had thought to ask what I'd do in the event that death came and took her from me. If only I'd prepared myself. I truly meant it when I told her I'd never leave.

I still mean it. Not that it matters much; she's dead and I can't get her back. If some creator means to stitch my soul back into one piece, these memories will surely pull the stitches apart. My soul or being, whichever you prefer, has split itself apart and innumerable questions are pouring out of the abyss.

It's time to exit the time machine for now. Anyone knows that spending too much time in a time machine is dangerous. Heaven knows I've spent too much time in mine. So much that I'm ready to end my life rather than live remembering any longer.

I've learned that most people never bother to construct time machines, or feel the need to otherwise relive the past in an intentional way. They are perfectly content to wander through life, seemingly unthinking. They're unaware of their constant and unending effort to suppress the despair they feel every day, the despair they feel at the impossibility of continuing to exist without knowing why they exist at all.

I know this because I lived like this.

Death shook me out of forgetfulness.   And now each and every thought is about what I don't want to think about anymore. Every thought is about my own death and when I'll have the courage to scrape the razor down my forearm and join my love in the great alone. There are fires, once put out, that can never reignite. There are wires, once frayed, which can never be restored. There are lines, once blurred, which can never be retraced.

I'm terrified as the warm pine and alcohol lull me into sleep. I'm terrified that even if I manage to piece things back together, the cracks and marks of grief will ruin my mind for the rest of my life.

CHAPTER 2

It's a strange realization that I desire nothing at all. It's obvious that any desire, fulfilled or not, amounts to nothing. It doesn't bother me at all. I'm keeping this in mind as I head into town for breakfast. My choices for wining and dining are limited in the Tennessee deep and it's taken some adjusting to get used to restaurants and stores closing at nine.

As a child I was told to give thanks to God for the small things. I feel no obligation to give thanks to a "creator," since it's apparent that I'm none the better off with or without these small things. I'm none the better off breathing than not breathing. Reluctantly I admit to unconsciously giving thanks for rum and coke, but I don't direct that gratitude toward a higher power.

I'm fuming at the possibility that this reality I'm living in could be some sick game orchestrated by a bored God as I walk into Maggie's Café. Maggie's is more or less a large workshop shed fitted with a kitchen, a bar, and a dozen tables. A dozen heads swivel and stare at me as I enter. I try and keep my eyes down, knowing that should I make eye contact with some poor bloke, I'll be unable to hide my disdain for the backwoods nation that these patrons seem to represent.

An attractive young lady seats me. Her nametag reads Maraye. I feel a twinge of guilt move within me as I subconsciously do a double-take. She has jet-black hair and porcelain white skin. All of her features are stark in comparison to each other.

Her eyes are like the jungle, filled with green. Her frame is small, hair pulled back in a ponytail. Graceful and green is all I see. This is the first time in months I've paid attention to another human at all. It bothers me.

"Hello there, what can I get for you?" she asks brightly.

I think I sound startled when she asks for my order.

"Just bacon and eggs, please," I say, trying not to make eye contact. I'm normally too apathetic to care much about attractive females but she makes me feel oddly self-conscious. She has a sweet voice, calm and reposed.

"How do you want your eggs?" she asks.

"Sunny side up, please."

"What do you want to drink with that?" She speaks like she's never told a lie, with a tone that seems both wise and naïve all at once. Though she is making eye contact and is paying careful attention to my order, she seems to be far off in thought, maybe daydreaming.

"Can I get a boilermaker?" I ask casually. I don't mean it but I want to get her attention. I have oodles of charm when I want to hook someone. It works. Her head snaps up and she finally notices me.

"What? It's nine in the morning," she says, looking harder at me.

"I'm kidding. Can I just get water please?"

She's still looking at me. She seems to be on the verge of speaking but hesitates. Finally it dawns on me. I recognize the familiar pity I've seen in others' eyes. It's always the pity.

"Yeah, I'll be back in a minute." I'd like to disappear when she looks at me like that with furrowed brows.

"Thanks."

"No problem," she says, walking back to the kitchen.

The poor thing is fighting that southern accent for all she's worth. I watch her legs walk toward the kitchen, her facial expression one of stone. She is very lovely; I'd put her around my age, in her mid-twenties. She's got looks that should be framed, with her soft, midnight black hair and porcelain skin, bright red lipstick and high cheekbones. She doesn't seem to enjoy being here. Despite her kindness, she seems bored, almost like she's walking around on autopilot.

Lenai's memory pulls me back to my usual plane of thought. She too, walked alive at some time, just like the waitress who'd disappeared into the kitchen. Her voice and the thought of enduring this remembrance for a lifetime have my forehead firmly on the table by the time Maraye's footsteps approach my table.

"You alright?" Maraye looks down at me like I'm a stray dog. She sets my plate on the table. I can feel the saline burning my eyes but the river doesn't flood.

"Yeah, thanks, just a little worn out, that's all. I haven't slept much lately." I don't understand why I'm explaining myself to this stranger.

She looks hesitant to speak and a frown forms; her eyes are grim in a way. They're salty and downcast. They make me wonder if she too has seen the terrible truth, that we must either be stupidly unaware or live in despair. There is no exit. There is no truth. There is nothing that death does not destroy. I rub my hands across my face. I haven't always thought this way about life. Life was just life. It was just all right.

"I think you know my grandpa. Are you Emmett?"

"Your Grandpa?" I ask.

She has that "oops" look painted on her face. She reluctantly explains.

"Yeah. Sorry. My grandpa is your landlord. He told me about you. I figured it was you since I didn't know you and I know everyone from this redneck town."

"Mr. Locke? He's your grandpa? He's very kind," I say, smiling politely.

"Yeah, he told me you're always drinking at the marina. I guess he thinks you drink too much. I get it, though. I'm sure you have your reasons. I told him there's not much else to do out here when you're our age."

"Oh man, is he going to kick me out?" I ask, a little surprised that the old man had noticed my drinking.

"No," she laughs. "He just feels bad for you living out there all by yourself."

"Oh," I say. "How does he know I drink? I don't drink for fun or anything."

"He picks up your empty bottles down at the marina."

"Oops," I say, feeling like an idiot. "I'm sorry about that. I'll pay more attention."

"He doesn't mind. He has this thing about taking in strays. He worries about you. It's one thing to be young and drunk, he says. It's another thing to live alone in a cabin and be drunk all alone. He doesn't like to see people by themselves. He never has," she explains, efficiently swiping a nearby table with a rag as she speaks.

"What do you mean?" I ask, really curious.

She stops pushing the rag around and shifts her weight to the back of her heels. I think she's as confused about what's happening as I am. I don't converse with other people, and she doesn't seem comfortable speaking with a total stranger about his personal life, either.

"I just mean, why on earth would anyone as young as you live alone in this crap hole? Happy young boys don't live alone in the woods. They spend their time in the city trying to get laid and make money."

I laugh hard which makes her laugh. "You're observant," I chide. "Your grandpa has been very kind to me. I'll be more respectful."

"I know he is and it's fine. I promise. I tell him all the time that he was a saint in another life," she says, smiling with the look of someone who is content in her grandfather's adoration.

It makes me smile to think Mr. Locke pays more attention to me than he lets on. I'm still human after all. It also strikes me as strange that I haven't noticed Maraye before now. I'm not sure how I feel about that, but I don't give it much thought. As arrogant as I am about my breadth of knowledge in my field of study, I know that if I were to study every book on abstract sciences and metaphysics, I could never understand human beings.

Still grinning, I offer an appreciative thank you when she returns with my breakfast. Her smile makes me think she's warmed to me. I like conversing with Maraye. I didn't realize how nice conversation is until now. I've missed it more than I knew.

The green in her eyes mangles my mind. It sets fire to my thoughts. I glance up from the table; she's still standing here. Her dress is so damn blue and her eyes ... she's looking at me, waiting to see if I speak. When I fail to find words, she kindly fills the silence.

"Do you like it out here?" she asks, tucking her hair behind her hair. I wonder if that's a nervous habit.

"What's that?" I ask her, looking down at my plate. She's standing so close; it makes me feel euphoric and muffles my thoughts.

"Oh yeah," I say, her words catching up to me. "I like it well enough, I suppose. I like the cabin a lot. The woods are nice and the lake is quiet. Do you like it here?" I ask as I finish my eggs. I'm genuinely interested to know.

"It's alright, I guess," she responds, looking amused. "It's not quite as charming for me. I've been stuck here my entire life."

"Why haven't you left?" I ask.

"I won't leave my grandpa here by himself," she says, looking away with what looks like a little bit of self-consciousness, suggesting she's as uncomfortable as I am. But she continues "We don't have family around here. It's just the two of us."

"What about your parents? Don't you have any brothers or sisters?"

In the back of my mind I'm baffled that I'm taking such an interest in her. To think so intently about someone besides myself gives me a feeling of relief and a welcome break from my unending self-consciousness.

"It's just us," she says with a trace of bitterness. "Anyway," she adds, clearly changing the subject, "What have you been doing out here, for fun, or whatever?"

"I spend all my time walking around in the woods, drunk out of my mind, in the middle of nowhere, Tennessee."

I'm joking and I think she can tell because I laugh and smile at her. Unfortunately the truth hidden in my words takes a hold and begins to drag me back to the familiar ache.

She's looking at me with that look, that same look she had earlier, when she realized I am the drunk her grandpa talked about. I hate it. I hate the pity but it's evident that she sees through my joking words.

"I'm sorry," she says, trying to ease the tension. "It's not my business. We don't have to talk about that. I was just asking because I thought you might want to hang out sometime or something, if you get too bored or whatever. I'm sorry. I don't normally ask strangers to hang out. Actually I never ask anyone to hang out. You just … I don't know … you seem nice and my grandpa likes you."

"No thanks. I'm not a stray dog." My own voice sounds much harsher than I intend to be, but it hurts to think of being around a female who isn't Lenai.

"Listen…" she starts up. The look on her face has me feeling painfully repentant. I might be a broken down car but I'm not cruel. I don't treat people like this.

"I didn't mean for it to come out that way. I just like being alone. I'm sorry. Please, I didn't mean to sound like that," I explain, pleading for forgiveness with my eyes.

"It's alright," she responds. "Let me know if you change your mind though, I like that cabin you're living in a lot. I used to go there with my mom. I miss it. I haven't been since she died." Her voice is full of reverie. I understand it all too well.

"You're an orphan?" I ask.

"No, my dad's just an ass. He lives in California. My mom died last year from cancer. We got along. I was lucky to have a good mother. Anyway," she says, "I've got to get back to work. See ya' around."

It hurts to see her walk away, and it hurts worse to recognize the guilt I've inflicted upon myself by talking to her, but then also by refusing her. It might not kill me to invite her over, but there is the possibility that it could. Our eyes meet when I get up to leave and she meets me with a half-smile. I smile and nod at her, still feeling the sting of my harshness.

On the drive back to my cabin I think of Maraye. I can't help but imagine what it would be like to socialize with her, even just over dinner at the cabin. It's been nearly a year since I last shared a meal with another person, but a girl like that deserves someone whose wires aren't worn and frayed.

"That's the end of that," I think to myself.

I push her from my mind as I turn onto the gravel road leading down to my cabin. The guilt from thinking so hard on Maraye is strangling me. I get drunk and doze off.

After a few hours I wake up and stumble to the marina. It's hard to pick up my feet so I drag them and trip on the steps into the docking area. The marina is more or less a small metal port for a dozen boats at the end of the driveway leading to my cabin. My own Jon boat is sheltered beneath it. Mr. Locke told me it came with the house. I lower myself down next to it and let the water graze my shoes.

My reflection in the water is a stark reminder of my condition: despondent and bleak. I realize my physical appearance is beginning to mirror the state of my insides. Hollow green eyes look back at me. The water reflects unshaven cheeks, unkempt black hair and sagging eyelids I don't recognize as belonging to myself. I imagine slipping over the edge and slowly sinking away.

All along it was right in front of my face: love anyone at all and you run the risk of outliving him or her. A sick, unavoidable game of Russian roulette that all mankind is forced to play and which most of us refuse to acknowledge we are participating in, even to ourselves. I find myself wishing Lenai had never existed at all. I've lost my love and if I don't find the will to kill myself I'll spend the rest of my life seeking forgetfulness.

The great backwardness of it all is that remembrance brings the same agony that forgetfulness brings. This goes back and forth, and on and on in my mind, each and every moment. Does Lenai's consciousness still exist? Do I believe that after I die I'll continue to exist? Am I already dead? How far does the love I vowed unending really go? Am I selfish for following her into forever by committing suicide? Or would that be the ultimate proof of a selfless love?

When a person can no longer accept the impossibility of resolving the meaning of life, is that true death? If it is, I am very much dead already. This is what pulls me so near to suicide. The more I think about killing myself, the more I yearn for a further shore reunion with my loved ones. Yet I've been unable to end myself, unable to escape the thought that I might be missing something. It wasn't until Lenai's death that I realized the inadequacy of my thoughts. I was arrogant and drunk with love. I was young. I thought I could trust my mind and the thoughts that it generated. I'm still young, though now I don't feel that way.

It seems impossible to me that I can hope for anything beyond what I can see and feel in this moment without having faith in God. But faith for the purpose of consolation is not genuine and is void of meaning. If I should come to some kind of faith, it will not be a cheap faith. I'm aware that I'll only accept an intellectually defensible faith. That's something I don't think I'll ever find.

If only I had the willpower to make up a faith in some tribal flag-waving God. I could merely find comfort in a God of self-image and fool myself into a sense of certainty and security. No, I can't trick myself into faith; all my efforts have failed, and the childhood indoctrination has worn out. I turn my thoughts to science and logic.

Before Lenai's death I was attending school. I was an aspiring theoretical physicist. My love for science is likely where my pride stems from; now I have to resist the urge to scoff at those who seek comfort outside the scientific realm. I abandoned my studies after her death, floating around the world on my grandpa's life insurance benefits. I had always used my understanding of the physical universe as a way to freeze over hell and ignore the afterlife.

Science is a pretender; though I adore it, it is no good to a man in despair. It can provide a how, but rarely a why. It's cruel and provides no true comfort for someone like me. Cruelty is a God building me a house, inviting me in, locking the windows and doors, and setting it ablaze. If there really is a creator, I can't help but see him as a master torturer. He must find the inevitability of despair highly amusing.

What if Lenai is off with this sadistic maniac right now, in some other life, alone and confused? How can I know one way or another if existence continues after death? If it does, what does that mean for life on earth?

Some say that God is good and that I should not despair the dead. Well, either God does not exist or he is not the kind creator they paint him to be. I saw what he did to her while she was here with me. I saw how her time ended and it was not in goodness.

Of course, my human perception is so skewed I recognize that I could be viewing his supposed goodness through a distorted lens. At the very least, I find comfort in the knowledge that I am here enduring this confusion and pain, and not her.

That's precisely why I flood with guilt whenever I find myself in enjoyment of anything. That's why my encounter with Maraye feels like a curse. I don't mind that I'm here suffering and Lenai isn't. But when the suffering breaks, even for the smallest fraction of a moment, I feel I am sliced to shreds. It feels like a betrayal.

The failing sun makes it easy to slip into that familiar sickness of suppressed memories triggered by scent and sound. I play a game in my mind, closing my eyes and choosing to make-believe the reality I choose. Lenai is sitting next to me now, her feet gracefully skimming the water. I'm halfway trying to pull myself back before I slip too far into the delusion, but the will is not there. I want to make-believe that she's here with me. The alcohol helps me conjure up her phantom.

I've stumbled into a place that I shouldn't go. My love for her is one that never refuses her – not even her phantom. Too often I find myself staring out into the woods, listening to her voice in my mind.

"She's not here," I whisper to myself, trying to think rationally. "Let me go," I plead, but the image of her ghost is so clear in front of me. "You're dead," I tell her. "You're not coming back."

She doesn't say a word and just stares at me, smiling. I lay here curled like a fetus. The world is silent except for my stifled sobs. Finally my mind wins out and I force the delusion to end. She gets up to leave, making her way across the lake back into the forest.

I crawl to the edge of the dock, lean over the edge and look down at my unfamiliar reflection. Salty tears flow down my cheeks, over my chin and into the water. The force of the drops makes tiny ripples in my image on the water. There's nothing left of the boy who spent his days happy and whole in Brooklyn. I am seeing myself more clearly than I did even minutes before: my hair is shoulder length, black as the lake in the moon's absence. It reeks of liquor. When I look at my eyes in the reflection it doesn't seem like anyone's home.

I don't want to live anymore. I'm weary of unending nights like these, unyielding and agonizing. The pain is overcoming my cowardice and in moments I feel I finally have the courage to set myself free. I take a deep breath, and pull myself closer to the edge of the dock. I close my eyes and let go. The impact of my body hitting the water is devastating. It's a cold I've never known before. The icy water constricts my breath, speeding up the asphyxiation.

I'm barely floating. The cold makes it nearly impossible to swim. But the freezing water has broken through the drunkenness and I struggle unwillingly. Regardless, I'm slowly drowning. The water numbs my body and I taste saline on my lips as I feel myself sinking down below the surface and into the murky abyss. The clouds break a bit and the moon shows dimly through the surface.

Sounding only in my head, I try and talk to God.

"Why'd you take her from me?" I scream as my head breaks the surface. My lungs are burning, filled with flames. I wait for a miracle. I'm a little child holding my breath to get my way. My hands flail uncontrollably. I feel my hand smack the solid metal of the dock and I wrap my hand around it, pulling myself to the side. The pain is too extreme. I drag myself down the side of the marina through the water.

Somehow I pull my body through the weeds and wash up on shore, trembling and defeated. Unable to move, I look across the lake to the forest. There are no phantoms emerging through the dark, no ghosts offering forgiveness. I feel two and a half ruined decades behind me. I lie defeated on the shore and wait for my miracle. It doesn't come.

So it goes for what feels like hours, the wet and cold bringing me back to a memory before I arrived in Paris. I was on my way to Baltimore for Lenai's memorial service, staring blankly at the highway in front of me, preparing myself to see her one last time. But the waves of grief poured and poured over me until I was overcome at last.

I thought I could feel her beside me as I jerked the steering wheel on the empty highway, sprawling and sliding and skidding and bouncing and flipping on the roof while it slid into the median, spinning and shattering into oblivion.

Obviously I didn't die. I failed to end myself. It's just another painful and embarrassing mistake. I'm unable to join my love - alone in the alone. The glass shattered, the windows blew out and sprayed me, and more and more waves of pain came pouring in as I hung upside down, spinning across the asphalt. Looking back it may have served me well to remove my seatbelt before I attempted suicide by car crash.

It finally ended. I just hung there dizzy and cold in the rain. Shards of glass fell from my hair. I felt a warmth on my arm and looked over to see blood slowly trickling down, diluted by the rainfall. I shed no tears. I made no sound. I simply stared out the shattered windshield and watched a truck pull off to the side of the road. The driver was talking on a cell phone. He must have been calling an ambulance. Not long after, a few cops showed up.

Lowering myself, I heard one of the cops yelling for me to be still and remain where I was. I ignored him and crawled through the shattered glass. He screamed louder, running toward me.

"I have to get to Lenai," I sputtered, sliding through the grass and mud before things went black again.

I woke to the scent of fluid in my nose. It took me a few moments to adjust my eyes to the luminescent lights above me. The morphine was surging through my veins. My neck tensed as the medicine carried me into blissful forgetfulness. A nurse's voice broke through my awareness, telling me to lie back and relax; the morphine didn't give me a choice. I tried desperately to surface.

"I have to get to Lenai," I said, grabbing her arm.

"I'm sure she'll be here as soon as she can. Just relax," she told me. I didn't have time to explain to her before I drifted off into my morphine-induced coma.

I remember seeing Lenai's face in front of mine while I slept in the hospital. We were dancing in the park. The time machine lurched backward again; the painkillers urged the dreams on and on. Before I awoke I was dreaming of our camping trip to Oregon. I could see the two of us asleep beneath timber.

I was angry when I woke up, minus most of the morphine, in the hospital; I wanted to stay sleeping with Lenai in my dream world. I had three broken ribs and a slight concussion, stiches on my left side where some glass stabbed through, but consciousness hurt more than the physical pain.

A few days later, Lenai's mother, Sonya, arrived and sat with me in the empty hospital room. She didn't ask how the wreck happened. I'm convinced that she knew. She's aged well, a sweet, pretty woman in her forties. We weren't very well acquainted but I could tell that she cared very deeply for me.

"You didn't get to say goodbye to her with the rest of us, Emmett," she said, tearing up.

I was uncharacteristically open with her, mostly influenced by the euphoric effect of the medicine in my I.V. "I don't want to say goodbye. I want to be with her."

Sonya reached across my bed, wiping my hair from eyes. She smiled at me, full of pain and remorse. The wounds were so fresh then, I could hardly breathe through the grief.

"She was happy with you, Emmett. Did you know that? She told me the things the two of you did together, how respectful you were, and how much she loved you. Did you know that?"

"We loved each other," I whispered, grabbing my skull in my hands, gritting my teeth. I'm not comforted. I'm angry. I want to scream and rip the room apart.

She took a tissue to her face, softly crying into it. "Not many people get to leave this life as happy as she was. I wanted to thank you for that." "Why did this happen?" I asked her quietly, pushing the call button for my nurse to come and administer more painkillers. I was in relatively little physical pain but wanted to self-medicate with anything I could.

"You know, Emmett, I'm a woman of faith. I have my moments of anger but I happen to believe that there's hope for all this mess. I hope that maybe it can all be restored, that it's not just an accident. Do you have faith?"

Her faith was just psychosomatic comfort in my eyes. But I don't have it in me to rid her of her hope.

"No. I want to but I can't find it."

"Well, I hope you find it, sweetheart. It's a terrible fate to live a life without hope. Lenai wouldn't want that for you," she said, hugging me gently.

I was discharged from the hospital a few days later. I never returned to New York. My lease was paid up for the year so I rented a car and met Sonya in Baltimore. She gave me Lenai's old jeep. It was her idea. My insurance company reimbursed me what they thought my car was worth. It wasn't a lot. I had to pay for some new parts on the jeep but a few days later I said goodbye to Sonya and drove west. I was halfway to Paris when I remembered my grandpa fondly recalling his childhood on the lake. That's how I ended up here.

Early on I would sit in the jeep and drink because I could still smell Lenai in it. Now the scent has faded. More and more, every day, she slips further away. All I have now are memories and make believe.

The dreary quiet follows me into the cabin. My breathing returns to normal as I rest in a hot shower to ward off my hypothermic state.

CHAPTER 3

I am never going to get rid of the vision of her face before my eyes. Every few days I awake, strangely confused. It's as though I can see Lenai on a projector screen lying next to me. I see the corpse of my love shining beautiful beneath the moon, and we lie together in a bed of shattered glass. I hear the screeching of tires and for a few moments it's as though it is happening now and I think the part of me that knows those moments are in my imagination thinks I'm coming unhinged.

After awakenings like this one, I'm not sure our love was worth this suffering. If I'd only refused her love, she'd likely be alive, happy and whole. It was my weakness that put her where she was when she died.

All of my answers and hopefulness depend on the afterlife or lack thereof. Am I a spiritual being, and if I am, what now that my purpose has forever fled? Where do I go, now that my home has imperceptibly vanished into nothingness? All of this leads to a longing for just one delusion to stick, to permeate my consciousness, so that I may escape from the endless questions and pain.

The deluded thoughts begin to ring out from my mind. "God, if you are there…" I hear my brain saying.

It's not unusual that I find myself trying to connect with a God, with something that can give me answers. The grass dampens the hem of my jeans while I trudge alone, trying to bargain with a God who isn't listening. I want God to be there, to offer an alternative to this inevitable ending.

"Please God," I hear my voice saying, aloud now, "repair the damage I've done. I want a backward forgetfulness, a joyous forgetting of myself. I am happy to disappear, to forget the ghosts I fear."

This goes on and on, the futile prayers of a lost child bouncing all over the shoreline as I walk to my jeep. The insomnia has rendered me a sleepless drunk, only resting during small naps sporadically throughout the days. I mostly sleep to ward off hangovers.

It's not yet sunrise as I head through the mountains, skimming Kentucky Lake, and across I-24. Some fear restrains the traveler within me, holding it at bay. *One day*, I think to myself, staring into the passing woods. One day I'll go into the woods and never come back.

These moments of aimless freedom help clear out the thick haze of thought. The gray dawn reflecting the fog skipping across the lake is like nature's morphine. Scenes like these provoke moments of pure ecstasy. They temporarily numb the anguish. I cruise dumbly through the mountains, accountable to no one. Fugazi blares through my speakers. Pick scrapes and distortion quiet my mind.

The trees and waterline behind them remind me of camping with Lenai in the forests of Oregon. We woke up on the cold ground, our cheeks covered in dew, the sun warming us through the trees. In that flawless awakening I felt love tearing through me. I opened my eyes to see her face, calm and at peace. My happiness blotted out any fears I might have had. That morning is gone forever.

The jeep falls silent as I park at a scenic view and take a trail into the forest. As I wander through the woods, the trees bend and sway, murmuring a windy lament for the lonely boy, lost and alone in the cold, not-quite-death. The world grows silent, mirroring my long, blank pause in thought, accompanied with sighs heard by no one. The ground is stiff in the cold darkness of pre-dawn.

"This is a lovely place to die – so many spots to choose from," I whisper as I roll up my tattered jacket beneath the roots of an enormous yellow poplar and lay down between them.

It's no time at all before I am dozing. The delusions begin again. I see her silhouette drifting between the trees. It's all in my head and I know I make it up myself. I think I do this because I'm afraid of forgetting what she was like. Someday I won't remember her. I'll forget her face, her scent, her touch and the taste of her make-up. It terrifies me more than anything that I'll forget what she was really like and I'll be forced to make things up. I'll have to choose how I remember her, knowing it's mostly inaccurate. I want to kill myself before that happens. I'm just afraid that she won't be waiting for me when I kill myself. I don't know if it's better to live and remember as long as I can or if I should take the risk and hope I find her in whatever's next after life.

Phantom Lenai drifts through the gray and lies face to face with me. In my mind I beckon her to me. I'm desperately trying to stop doing this to myself. I really am. I know it's unnatural and unhealthy. Life with Lenai is over forever. But I can't stop myself. These bite marks are deep in my arteries. I swear I feel her breath between her teeth when I make believe the sound of her voice.

"If you stop all this nonsense, you'll sleep better won't you? Maybe you'll find some peace and you won't dream at night. Stop roaming to find a little bit of comfort and it might become quiet in your mind. Maybe you'll get out from under the pain you're drowning in."

Phantom Lenai's voice is really my own sinking back to me, trying to give myself advice, I realize.

The woods are eerily silent, save only for my sobbing. It feels as though all is breaking inside of me. I'm always most desperate in the morning.

"Just stay here with me a bit longer," I say to phantom Lenai as I shift to my back and stare up at the dim light cutting through the branches. I'd do anything for her to be here with me. I'd do anything to be intact.

I continue my delusional waltz with the past and pull a folded picture from my jacket pocket. It's a picture of Lenai and me at Coney Island. She snapped it quickly one evening as we were walking together. Her hair rests on her shoulders. She's wearing a white dress with a green peter pan collar. It was my favorite. She'd been annoying me for days about getting a picture of us and I'd refused. She took this picture three days before she died.

All this thinking about death is getting old but I suppose it's the only natural thing to do in suffering. I never thought much about life or death before Lenai. I'm ashamed of my indifference to the suffering around me.

I've had enough of sifting through pictures and memories so I stand and make my way back to my jeep. It feels like I've been in the forest for hours but it's just now dawn as I drive back to my cabin. I want to get home and drink until I black out. I want the aching to stop and I want to sleep and see Lenai's face.

Even through my drunkenness I can tell that it's a sublimely beautiful morning as I sit dozing on my front porch. I'd been making my way through some essays by Nobel Prize recipient, Albert Camus, before my chin dropped and I started drooling on them. I must have dozed for an hour or so.

I can see how sublimely beautiful Maraye looks when she pulls up in the driveway and steps out of her car. I'm not prepared for this in any regard. It's seven in the morning and I am drunk. I'm an unshaven abomination. She looks nervous as hell as she walks toward the porch biting her lip.

"What are you doing here?" I ask with an unintentional cruelty. "Sorry," I say covering my tracks. "I meant hello."

She raises her eyebrows at me, smirking.

"Hey there, I was hoping you'd be awake. Are you busy today?" she says, as though she were reciting lines. I'm assuming she rehearsed this before she arrived.

"No but I'm not really in the best state to entertain company," I say gruffly.

She glances at the bottle sitting in my lap and her eyes narrow. "Are you drunk Emmett? It's not even eight in the morning. Grandpa wasn't kidding. Were you like this before you moved out here to live alone like a crazy person?"

"No, I'm fine." I stand and try walking toward her. I miss the porch step and fall face first, cutting my face on the edge of a step. I hear her squeal in front of me as she moves toward me.

"Emmett! What the hell are you doing?"

"Maraye," I say, on my stomach, "I retract my previous statement. I think I'm slightly intoxicated."

I roll on my back and look up at Maraye. She's trying to hide her laughter with a look of concern. She's absolutely gorgeous in the morning sun. Her green sundress blows slightly in the wind, accenting her eyes.

"Good God, I don't even … you need to clean this," she says motioning to my cheek. "Come on, I'll take you to the pharmacy. Jesus Christ."

"No thanks. It's a scratch." I stand up and wipe my cheek with my sleeve. I balance myself with my hand on the porch floorboards and sit down, looking at her. She moves to join me.

"Emmett," she starts in a confused tone. "Why are you drunk? Have you slept?"

"Relax," I respond. "I'm more sober than drunk, I think. I slept for a while yesterday. I'm just on a strange sleeping schedule lately."

The worry in her expression nearly makes me feel guilty. My stomach drops like some pre-adolescent kid at a school dance. She furrows her brow as she glances once more at the whiskey across from me.

"I was just driving by, so I thought I'd stop in and see what you're doing today. I thought you might like some company. Are you always like this?" She bites her bottom lip and raises her eyes at me when she finishes.

"I haven't really had much of a reason to be decent. I'm sorry. Besides, it's so early. Normal people are sleeping right now. What would you have done if I were sleeping?"

She laughs, looking embarrassed. "If I'm being honest, I think I kind of just planned on driving by without stopping, but you ruined that."

I feel ashamed of my poor state. In my life before this I'd always prided myself on my ability to remain in a concise, proper state of mind, controlling my emotions.

"Listen," I start up. "Oh shit, I'm a mess." I move quickly to wipe all the dirt off my clothing and hurriedly try to tame my hair.

Maraye laughs and reaches for my hand, motioning me to relax. Instinctively I jerk away but she pretends not to notice.

"Hey, it's alright. Maybe you should take a shower and spend a day with a lonely girl. It could be good for you." Her green eyes drill into me. She is terrifying.

"Really, I'm not in the best state of mind. I'm a mess and I haven't slept," I say apologetically. I'm not lying. I'm horrified that this is happening and that I lacked the adequate time needed to prepare my mind.

She purses her lips at my response. She isn't taking no for an answer. "Emmett, hang out with my today or I'll have my grandpa evict you."

"What? No you won't. Will you?" I think I sound a little more panicked than I intend to sound. She starts to laugh. Her response echoes the innocence in my eyes.

"I didn't mean that." She's laughing and it makes me smile. "You're not such a cold-hearted bastard, are you? Please just be with me today."

I don't understand why she's so adamant about being with me but I intend to find out. "Yes, I am but okay, but let me get cleaned up. Jesus fucking Christ."

Her laughter echoes as I move toward the front door. I just shake my head.

I can't refuse her. There's a shortage of will power when our eyes meet. The way she looks at me makes me feel as though I'm having heart palpitations. She's going to kill someone with those looks someday. I'm sure of it. I open the door and ignore the alarms in my head sounding.

"Wait a minute. What can we possibly do out here?" I ask, turning to face her.

She looks at me with a smirk on her face. Her eyes are wide and bright now. I'm going to get myself in trouble if I continue to stare at her. Even so, I can't help but glance at her pale legs and collarbone.

"I was hoping we could fish. You know, you live on a lake and all," she says in a slightly sarcastic voice.

I can't help but laugh. "You're crazy. I don't know how to fish."

"That's alright, I can teach you …and we have a boat," she says, motioning toward the tiny Jon boat tied to the marina. "I'll get my gear out of the truck and get ready while you take a shower."

"Oh, okay," I stutter as I enter the cabin.

The shower sobers me up fairly well. I emerge from the cabin to find her waiting by the dock. I'm not used to seeing her. She's pale and frail in the morning sun. After a few hours and a trip to town we're finally ready to head out. I settle into the boat and push off from the dock, uncertain what to do with myself. There is no wind on the water. All is calm.

She breaks the silence. "Are you okay? You look kind of nervous."

"I'm alright. What are we fishing for anyway?" I ask, staring into the water.

"We're fishing for crappie. Grandpa taught me how. I'll show you how to set up some rigs for the pole holders behind you, and then you can cast one off to the side. I didn't think to pick up minnows so I guess we'll use jigs."

"I don't know what that is," I laugh, trying to break my uneasiness.

"That's okay. It's this thing here," she says, holding up and pink and orange-feathered piece of plastic attached to a hook. "Come over here and I'll show you how to tie it."

I stand and move slowly to the open space next to her. She laughs at me as I trip and grasp the side of the boat for balance. She demonstrates how to tie a knot with some fishing line and I mark her motions in my mind. When she moves her hand it grazes my knuckles and she smiles as I struggle to tie my jig to the line. I try to hide the shaking in my fingers from her.

"There you go … you got it," she says, her voice clean and sweet, and accompanied by a flawless smile. It frightens me that I'm so fond of her this quickly.

We float around the lake a while, mostly staying near stumps and submerged trees. She shows me how to navigate with a trolling motor. I'm mostly apathetic and it shows. As she fills the live well, she laughs at me as I struggle with the wire, consistently tangling it in my reel. Her constant staring makes me want to throw myself out of the boat and swim to shore. She makes me self-conscious. I don't like it.

"So what's your grandpa's story? Did you know your grandmother?" I ask.

Her face turns solemn but she recovers after a few seconds.

"I knew her when I was younger. I don't remember her very well. I mostly know her from grandpa's stories. He loved her very much. She died from cancer, the same as my mom. My mom and I were as close as we could be at my age. She worked a lot and my grandpa mostly raised me even back when she was alive."

"Have you ever had a boyfriend?" I ask.

Her face moves from solemn reverie to bitter and I regret prying, but she carries on despite my intrusion.

"Yes, I dated this guy for a couple of years. I never took it very seriously but I didn't know what else to do, especially in this crap town. I thought I was just going to have to settle for an asshole no matter what, so I tried to find the most bearable guy I could. It turns out that an asshole is an asshole and I learned my lesson when he started hitting me."

"Jesus, Maraye … I'm sorry, I shouldn't have …"

"It's okay," she cuts me off. "You want to know the worst part? Even though you've been rude to me, you showed more remorse in one look than he did the entire time I knew him. No one has ever apologized to me the way you just did."

"I'm sorry," I say again, handing her my pole to repair. "I know I'm cynical but I'm not like that at all. I promise."

"I can tell," she says handing my pole back to me. "At least I think I can. Anyway, it's my turn now."

"Okay, hit me," I laugh.

"Why did you come here?" She looks at me as though she's afraid I'll throw myself out of the boat. If she hadn't before now, she's definitely caught on to my discomfort now.

I take a deep breath and look at her.

"I don't really know. My grandpa liked it when he was younger. I guess it seemed like a good place to think about life. This seemed like a safe place for me to try and figure things out."

"What made you stop living life and start thinking about it so much?" she asks quietly, her eyes focused on what she's doing with her hands.

I want to try and steer the conversation away from me but I know I put her on the spot, so I need to pay my dues. I rub my hands through my hair and look hard at her.

"I was engaged to this girl and she died, so I took off," I say quickly.

"Fuck, Emmett, I am so sorry."

I can see on her face that she doesn't know how to respond and I don't fault her. There isn't much to do when a person drops that sort of bomb in a conversation. Her words have a rare kind of sincerity to them. I'm surprised at the comfort they bring.

"It's all right," I lie. "I'm over it."

"You don't have to pretend with me," she says with a pointed look.

"I don't?" I ask. I wonder if she's right.

"No, you don't. And between me and you, that's a pretty good reason to be drunk this morning."

I laugh and nod at her. We talk for a few hours. Maraye is pure gold. One of the most genuine souls I've ever known.

"Why did you come out here today? I'm a stranger," I ask at one point, a question that has been burning in my mind.

She looks at me, and then turns her gaze downward.

"Well ... When you come into the café, you just looked lost, I guess. You seem sweet to me, even though you can be really rude. You're always alone and somehow I just know you don't try to be rude. I just thought that since you're my age, maybe we could be friends. Even if it's just for today."

"Oh," I reply. It's all I can manage. I don't know what to say. I think she's lonely. I don't want her to be alone. I like her. But she couldn't have picked a worst candidate to alleviate her suffering. It's not in me to deny her sanctuary. Sadly I can't do much to improve her situation other than simply being around when I'm not completely out of my mind.

"Thanks," I say. "I think I've taken for granted how nice it feels to have a conversation."

She smiles and starts to respond, stops, and then starts up again. "If you don't mind me asking, what happened?"

"What do you mean?" I ask, even though I am fairly sure what she wants to know.

"I mean, how did she die?" she says softly.

I look up at Maraye. I'm not offended and I resign myself to control my emotions.

"Her name was Lenai. We were going to be married when we finished school."

"Oh," she says with a pained look. "I'm sorry. She must have been extraordinary. I mean you don't come off as the type of person who just settles for any girl you can get. You don't seem like someone who would be careless with their affection, I mean. Sorry," she laughs nervously. "I mean you seem mature. That's all."

It's strange to hear someone else speak of Lenai. I was beginning to think she was a figment of my imagination. The river floods and I grit my teeth as tears slide between my lips.

"She was extraordinary," I say, wiping my face. "I'll never be the same again. I'm sorry," I say, angry with myself for losing control. I breathe deep and compose myself. "I was very lucky to know her."

She smiles at me and stares out at the water. "I'm afraid," she says staring back at me. "I'm afraid I'll care about someone the way you cared about her and I'll lose them. The funny thing is that I've always wanted someone else to experience life with. You know … I guess like every stupid girl. I've always thought it would be worth the risk."

"That's not stupid," I tell her. "Everyone's looking for someone or something, I guess. It's only human."

"Do you think it was worth it?" she asks.

"I don't know," I respond sternly.

"Did Lenai get sick?" she asks, meeting my eyes. "Ignore that," she says quickly, dropping her head. "I'm sorry. I don't think before I speak. It's really none of my business."

"It's alright," I assure her. "I haven't been able to talk to anyone about my life in a long time. I normally feel awkward talking to other people, but I don't right now. She died on a drizzly Wednesday morning. We had been watching horror movies together … you know like normal kids, I guess, and I didn't want her to leave. I begged her to stay awake with me just a little longer. She didn't want to stay up too late because she had class the next morning, but she stayed with me anyway. We were awake all night. I think I cared more about having sex with her than what she required that night, which of course was sleep. That morning she was rushing to class because of me. The doctors told us that she had a tumor growing in her brain. It caused a seizure and she collapsed. A truck hit her in a crosswalk. It was my fault. I don't deserve to be here. She should be here."

I start to shake and struggle to regain control. It hurts to admit the truth aloud. There's no good way to recover myself but I try desperately to regain my composure.

"Listen … I'm sorry," I start up but she cuts me off.

"Don't do that," she says. "You don't need to be sorry with me. It wasn't your fault. I mean, you couldn't have known she had a tumor. I can't imagine carrying something like that with me."

My despair pushes me back into the dark. It feels as fresh as it ever has. I push toward her anyway.

"Thanks," I say. "I'm not like this. It's just actually nice to talk out loud to someone other than myself. It normally hurts to think about it, but it's not so bad with you. It's bad but not so bad."

"That's good to know," she replies. "Aren't we a funny pair? We're just damaged goods."

I laugh. "That's a good way to put it. F.U.B.A.R probably works just as well."

She laughs with me. "What is F.U.B.A.R.?"

"Fucked up beyond all repair," I explain.

She explodes with laughter and I grin hard and then laugh out loud. I hadn't thought about laughing at myself before this moment. It feels good, very good.

"Oh God, it's getting chilly. Do you want to head back now?" she asks, her slender arms wrapped around her torso.

"Sure," I say, subconsciously feeling a tug of despair that we might part ways so soon.

We take our time heading back to the marina to tie off the boat. I'm relieved when Maraye sits with me in my familiar spot on the shore of the lake. The moon is pushing through the cracks of the forest, making the water a pale green, and her bare legs a bright white. I listen to the hum of the wind crossing the surface of the water.

"Emmett ..." she whispers next to me. "I hope you can find what you're searching for out here."

Her words jar my mind. We're silent and I think about what I've really come out here to do. I've come out here to die. The cruelty and the irony are not lost on me. There are stars brighter than diamonds in the sky above us. The sun's completely gone now. Maraye's skin is as translucent as ever. We're snapped out of our quiet reverie by the sound of an engine behind us.

"Uh-oh," Maraye laughs. "It's my grandpa."

"What's he doing here?"

My nerves start to tense up.

"I told him I was coming here. I assume he came to join the party."

Maraye's calm puts me at ease as Mr. Locke pulls up in his pickup truck behind us. I feel a strange sorrow that my time with Maraye is interrupted. I haven't experienced this sort of bittersweet pain in a long while. As we walk toward Mr. Locke, she smiles at me and my legs tremble.

I hear his voice ring out up the driveway. "Hi, Maraye. Hi, Emmett. I just stopped by to see if you'd like to get some dinner. Come with us and let me buy you dinner, Emmett. I insist."

He's a gentle man; it's impossible to refuse sincerity like his or maybe I'm just not ready to leave Maraye. One more glance at her is enough to lure me in for good.

"Oh, alright," I say. "Thanks, Mr. Locke."

"Mr. Locke?" he asks, raising his eyebrows. "Please call me Jack. I'm not some boring old man."

Maraye laughs behind me as he ushers us to his truck. We're not on the road long before Jack starts making small talk. There's no escape.

"So, Emmett, how do you like the forest life? Is the cabin everything you dreamed it would be?"

"Truthfully, it's exceeded my expectations. I quite like the solitude."

He seems pleased with my response. Maraye takes her turn in our conversation dance. I'm aware of her arm lightly touching mine when the truck jostles on the crudely paved road.

"Grandpa, you'll never guess what Emmett did today. He caught some fish. They're still in the live well. We could have a cook-out tomorrow night. I don't have to work."

She looks over at me enthusiastically. I can't help but return her smile.

Jack laughs from the front seat. "We've already kidnapped the boy once, Maraye. I'm sure he's got things he'd like to do. Maybe another night," he says politely.

"Actually, that sounds nice, Jack. I mean … if you're free." I smile at Maraye. The way she lights up at my words makes me grin. I stare out the backseat window.

We get dinner at a small Italian restaurant across from The First Baptist Church of Paris. I watch out the window as a few dozen people scurry in for Wednesday night service. Most of the congregants are older, no doubt sobered up by tragedy after tragedy, searching for some kind of comfort.

We place our orders in silence. The restaurant is mostly quiet. The dim lighting is kind to Maraye's features. Staring at her lips I feel a burning sensation in my gut. I'm staring unintentionally and both Jack and Maraye notice. I hear her giggle and the reverie is broken. I'm certain my face matches her lipstick now. The smile forming behind Jack's gray beard suggests that he's amused.

Jack is not unlike my own grandfather. His gentle demeanor makes it difficult to maintain my usual sense of discomfort. Outside, a couple hurries by, laughing playfully and embracing. A vision of Lenai and I walking through Central Park pulls me back into the past. The familiar guilt swells and I find myself wishing for an escape. What am I doing with these people?

Across from us two teenage girls are seated. Within minutes I'm squirming in discomfort. One benefit of solitude is that I haven't had to endure the company of senseless mallrats in months. It's cruel to judge strangers but this suffering has made me less kind. To Jack's credit he doesn't seem to notice their high pitched ramblings. Looking over I notice the two of them are covered in nearly identical apparel. The current social convention in townie fashion must be to garb oneself in clothes adorned with tacky, diamond-studded crosses. I'm not sure why I focus so much on my disdain for their thoughtlessness about the reality of death and pain. I think I'm angry that they haven't been robbed of their unconscious naiveté.

The louder of the two is short and plump. She closely resembles a pug. She's been obnoxiously reliving a visit to some club in the city where she was apparently groped by a hulk of a man. It's the kind of disgusted rant that betrays she's actually pleased with herself. They appear to be in their mid-twenties. I find myself fuming. There's no excuse to be so unaware at their age.

Fortunately for my mind, Maraye's persona begins to calm me down as soon as I look at her. It's her presence that keeps me from leaping across the room and strangling them. Slowly the anger recedes and I feel guilty for judging complete strangers so harshly. I wonder why I feel so angry. Then I realize: I don't know their stories. Perhaps they have experienced pain, too. The point is, I have no idea. All I know is that their conversation is annoying and their clothing is appalling. I turn my thoughts back to Maraye and Jack and let it go.

"Hey Emmett," Jack starts out. "Did you know that the capybara is the largest rodent?"

"Grandpa!" Maraye laughs. "What the heck?"

"I've been watching that Discover Channel."

"Discovery Channel, grandpa," she corrects him, still laughing.

"Whatever. The thing looks like a baby hippo with hair. It's ugly as sin," he says, his eyes shining at Maraye.

I can't help but laugh.

"I love the Discovery Channel, Jack. I'm a bit of a scientist myself. I was going to be a physicist," I explain.

"A what? I thought you looked smart," he says.

Our laughter drowns out the incessant townie talk from the two aspiring reality television stars next to us.

"You were going to be a physicist?" Maraye asks, looking impressed. "What happened?"

She looks at me apologetically the moment her words are out. My face falls and I can see that it crushes her. Jack feigns ignorance and rescues the conversation.

"What does a physicist do exactly?" he asks nonchalantly as he twirls his angel hair noodles around his fork. I'm grateful for his question. I smile at him, thinking of a way to explain it without sounding like an arrogant know-it-all.

"They try to figure out how nature works," I say.

"Oh, is that all?" He smirks at me jokingly. "Do they ever figure it out?"

"Sometimes, but it takes time and trial and error. It's mostly asking life's hardest questions and then seeking answers, even though it seems impossible most of the time," I explain, remembering why I love physics.

"What do they call people who try to figure out the 'whys' of life?" he asks, raising his eyebrows.

"Oh, those fools are lovers and poets," I answer, chuckling.

He smiles at me thoughtfully.

"You know, I think you might be all of the above Emmett. You have a very poetic way of speaking for a young man."

He's right. I am foolish. I'm a fool for agreeing to all of this today. I'm an idiot for letting myself get dragged away from my thoughts of Lenai. This may be the longest period of time I've gone without thinking of her. The guilt pours over me. This is a new feeling, a different kind of guilt. I hate myself for enjoying the company of these people so much. I don't deserve it.

Without realizing it, I find myself staring back across the street at the church and its congregants. The latecomers hurry inside.

"That's where Maraye and I go on Sundays," Jack says, noticing my gaze. "You're welcome to join us this Sunday, if you like."

I think to myself that there's no chance in hell I'll set foot inside a church but I lie to Jack.

"Sure, I'll let you know if I'm up for it sometime." He's not an idiot. I can tell by the look in his eyes that he sees through my lie but lets it go.

We spend the rest of our meal talking about town happenings and stories of Maraye's childhood. Jack and Maraye are kind and charming. I'm careful not to look directly at Maraye when I can help it. Nevertheless, temptation wins out every few minutes and I look up to see her smiling at me each time.

I'll have to leave her beauty behind. It's inevitable. I fled out here to find answers and finish myself off. It would be cruel to risk Maraye's heart when my own is no longer intact. She shouldn't have to see what's likely to become of me at the end of this tale. I'm a dead star to her. She sees me here, burning, alive and drawing breath, but I've been dead for a long time. She just doesn't know it yet.

When we arrive back at the cabin Maraye and I bid Jack farewell. She lingers a moment next to me, clasping her hands

"Well, I'll walk you to your car," I say.

"Actually I was hoping you'd want to drink some tea before I head home," she says quickly.

I look up to see her biting her bottom lip in a way that makes me shake. I make a mental note that she does this often, especially when she's nervous.

"I don't have any. I'm sorry."

She laughs at me. "I have some in my car. I went to the store yesterday and never took it out."

"Oh, ok. That works," I say.

I watch her hurry to her car.

"It's sleepy time tea. Is that alright?" she calls.

"Yeah, I don't know what that is, but I'm sure I'll like it." I feel like an idiot shouting across the driveway to her.

A few minutes later I'm reluctant yet excited as I wait on the porch for her to bring out our drinks. The air is chilled but feels nice through my thermal. She comes out with one of my jackets wrapped around her. It makes me smile. She curls up on the swing and I sit with my back resting on a column.

It's a cloudless night. The cicadas seem louder than usual. It's possible that the rest of the forest is silent. I can't help but imagine the forest life creeping in, the trees bending and swaying closer to watch us, curious that the hermit boy from the cabin has company.

"The stars seem close tonight," she observes, breaking the silence. I let a grin slip out. I love talking about astronomy. It's been my passion since I was a child.

"You know, the sun is the closest star," I say, gazing up into the night sky.

"Really?" She asks with a smile. "I like the stars. They make me want to run free."

"That's funny; did you know they're in perfect balance? They're in constant conflict with themselves. The collective gravity of all the mass of a star is pulling it inward. If there were nothing to stop it, the star would just continue collapsing for millions of years until it became its smallest possible size."

She's laughing hard and I'm embarrassed. "I didn't know that." She's still laughing. "I don't know what that means," she confesses through her laughter.

"Oh," I say, feeling self-conscious. I have no real idea why I continue rambling but I do. I guess I want her to understand. "They make me think of people actually. If there weren't some 'thing' in us constantly nagging and tugging, trying to make us better and more decent, we'd just love and serve ourselves until we became very small people. There probably wouldn't be any humanity left in us; the same way a star with strong gravity becomes smaller and smaller until it's a black hole. It makes me wonder if a strong tragedy can chip away a person's heart until there's nothing left."

"I like your mind, Emmett." She smiles, looking at me from behind her cup of tea.

I drink deep from mine, feeling embarrassed about carelessly sharing my personal thoughts and wondering why I am. The chamomile calms and soothes my throat as it pours down. She's looking at me, and I get the feeling that she can feel the pain behind my talk of black holes and broken hearts.

"Why'd you abandon your studies?" she asks me. "It seems like you're a perfect fit for a scientist. I haven't seen you this excited to talk about something since I've known you."

The pain resurfaces when I think of the answer. "I don't know. I guess I lost the motivation. Mostly, it was hard to be in the city after Lenai's death. I guess I don't know what I could possibly do that death won't inevitably destroy."

The expression on her face paints a picture of pain and pity. "It's all on you to get yourself out from under that weight," she tells me. "You know you can't live like this forever. We need people."

"I know," I say, "I think I have a solution anyway." I don't mean to add the second half of that, and I'm instantly remorse-filled.

"What's your solution?" she asks.

"Nothing," I say, a little sharply. "I really don't think anything I do will bring my aspirations back to me. What's the point? Lenai isn't coming back."

"You can always choose to feel differently. You can't spend the rest of your life without anyone, or purpose, or love. Emmett, how old are you?"

"I'm twenty-two. I feel older though."

"Oh right, you're such an old man! I mean shit you're at least twelve months older than I am," she says with a sarcastic tone I haven't heard yet.

I snort my tea in my laughter and Maraye laughs with me as I struggle to wipe my face with my shirt.

"Ok, fine. Fair enough. I guess you're right. I am trying, though. I mean that's why I came out here: to find a way out."

She looks hard at me, putting her legs up on the arm of the swing. "Well, I hope you find a way out," she says with the tone of a hopeful lover. She stands up and I mirror her.

"It's late. I need to get home," she says, smoothing the skirt of her dress.

"Yeah," I say, "Um … well, I liked spending the day with you. It was nice to have company." I lower my voice, hoping she can feel my sincerity.

"I had a nice time with you," she says, biting her lip again. No force on earth can make me shake the way I do each time she does that. "When will I see you again?"

"Oh, I think soon. I'm going to New York in a few days to pick up some of my old things. But I'll be back. I'm not staying."

"Oh, but you're coming back, right? For sure?" Her fear stirs the remorse inside me.

"Yes, I'll only be gone a day or two. I don't want to linger there. I have no one to see," I add painfully. It's all I have in me to ignore the guilt threatening to choke me out.

Maraye leaves with my jacket wrapped around her. I pretend not to notice because I know she can use it as an excuse to come back to see me. It's nice having someone to talk to other than a ghost and myself. When her taillights disappear I walk down to the marina and look out at the stars, hoping for answers to fall and smack me in the face.

A part of me feels as though the answer I'm looking for just left and drove away. A new kind of loneliness rolls over me and I find myself wishing that Maraye were still here to talk with me.

CHAPTER 4

I am returning to my flat in Brooklyn to clear out my things. I've put it off for too long. Fortunately I'd used money from my inheritance to pay my year-long lease in full. My lease expires in two weeks, so I have no choice but to get what I want and leave the rest. I promised Maraye I'd return in one piece as soon as I could. I don't intend to linger here. I push the anxiety of returning to this place from my mind until I arrive at the airport.

It's not long before the old scents and sounds push me back into the time machine. I'm stepping off the L train when the reality of what I'm doing hits me hard. I struggle through the anguish all the way to my apartment. I breathe deep, slide the key into the lock and walk inside. Nothing could prepare me for this nightmare. Suddenly my losses are fresh again; every memory was waiting for me here in silence. Breathing deep I scan the rooms from left to right.

The mirror I shattered when Sonya called to give me the news is still spread across the dining room. A picture of Lenai and I still rests behind a magnet on the refrigerator. My intestines lurch and I vomit. I sit down on my abandoned couch. The scent of honey, vanilla and berries drifts through the air. It's Lenai's perfume. Sitting here reminds me of the days I'd spend waiting here for her to walk through at the end of a long day. It feels like I never left, like I'm still waiting here, like she went to pick up take-out so she could come back to our warm and safe home.

She's not here. She's not going to walk through the door ever again. I should stop thinking, stand up and grab what I want. It would be best for me to move quickly and leave without looking back. I blur out my thoughts and walk to the bedroom.

The bedding is disheveled, signs of the lovers who once lay there all over it. One of Lenai's blouses is hanging from the door. The mirror on the door reflects a ruined young man. I don't know myself anymore. It's completely silent as I curl up on the half of the bed where I once rested.

This is the last place I saw her alive.

Lenai's phantom joins me, lying next to me, looking in my eyes, silent and perceptible in my psychosomatic delusion. What was once a vibrant and life-filled home seems more like a mausoleum. I can still smell Lenai when I bury my head into her pillow. My hand grazes something underneath it and I pull out a piece of folded paper. It's her handwriting. We used to write each other letters and hide them. She must have left it for me the morning she left for class, hoping I'd find it when I awoke. Time stops as I unfold the paper. The outside reads *TO MY LOVE, EMMETT*.

EMMETT,

You may not realize it but you've broken my fall. I wouldn't be able to cope with my father's death if not for you. Knowing that you wait for me every day, just to see my face, blocks out all the noise that threatens to suffocate me.

If you don't feel the peace that you bring to me, I hope you do someday.

I love you Emmett, with all that is within me.

Yours,

Lenai

I curl up, trying to scream but my voice is stifled through my heavy breathing. My hands pull hard on my hair and I finally let loose my rage. I roll off the bed onto the hardwood floor and pull myself onto my knees, firmly planting my head against the wall.

"Fuck! Fuck! Fuck!" My saliva covers the wall in front of me. My hands grasp the drywall and I smash my head several times until a small trickle of blood flows down my forehead from my scalp. I continue yelling incoherently as I punch the wall, my knuckles opening and bleeding. The bedframe cracks as I lift it and slam it into the wall.

"Fuck! Fuck! It's just a fucking game to you, you stupid fuck!"

I'm not sure who I'm yelling at. God, I guess. It doesn't do any good. I find no comfort or relief when I finish. It's nearly an hour before I calm myself and wash my wounds in the bathroom sink. I'm lucky that none of my knuckles appear to be broken or fractured, and there's only a tiny cut at the base of my scalp.

It's strange. Her letter is almost a kind of unintentionally self-willed farewell. A part of me laments that I never expressed to her exactly how content and at peace she made me feel. My breathing calms as I walk through this old abandoned home. Old clothing and photos fill my bags and I sift through the broken glass thinking of the time Lenai bought groceries for me. It's the simple memories that seem to make me ache most.

My television rests on a mantle above a fireplace; it's surrounded by miniature owls and baby deer toy replicas that Lenai placed there. I remember the day she brought them over, grinning and laughing as she littered the apartment with her toys and pictures. It was one of the happiest days of my life. We belonged to each other.

I feel the temptation rise and spread through me. I think of ending myself right here. I left the razor in Paris. For a moment I consider drinking myself to death. Lenai's desire for me to feel peace stays my hand. It would be an injustice to her for me to succumb to the pain after finding her wish for my life. Lenai's letter is all that sustains me. I'm angry once again, feeling as though she somehow knew it would keep me from total self-destruction.

After a while I calm myself and regain complete control of my emotions. I try to put the scene in perspective. The harsh reality is that a young man just found a note left by a dead girl, whom he loved dearly. It feels like another goddamn joke. It's sickening and it takes all my willpower to let it go. In my mind I hear Maraye telling me to come back to her. The truth is that I miss her and this place feels hollow and full of death; it mirrors my mind. It scares the shit out of me.

I move about the house softly and reverently, gathering the last few things. The silence and darkness makes me feel as if I'm not really here. I'm an apparition in this place that represents another life. There's nothing left of the boy and girl who filled this place with love.

It strikes me as I continue sifting and sorting that I left so much behind in this place. These silly little everyday things feel so precious and sacred. Lenai's lipstick and mascara rest on the bathroom counter. I pick them up and squeeze them in my palms. I pull the photo booth picture of us from the refrigerator and place it in a bag with the other artifacts. She doesn't feel any closer. This place is yielding no peace, no answers, no relief and no epiphanies.

My flight leaves in the morning. I can either stay here and suffer through another sleepless night or go out and find something to occupy me until I need to get to the airport. God only knows what pushes me out the door, but off I go, looking back into my old home one last time. I want to be around other people, even strangers.

I saunter around Green Point for a little while and notice a long line outside one of the local shelters. An idea forms in my mind, partially born out of boredom and partially out of the desire to understand what seems to be a kind of thick haze separating those who roam the city in the day and those who roam it at night. J. Michael Stracynski called it the Midnight Nation and the Daylight Nation. The wealthy family men, the stock brokers and bankers of the day are replaced by junkies, drunks and the mentally diseased at night. I feel a great swell of pity for these poor souls. I've never seen myself in them until now, but I'm without a home, I'm no different than them. We're more alike than not, I suspect.

Aside from having money, tonight I'm just as lost and tattered as they appear to be. I'll hole up in an alley and see what I can learn from them. I wonder if they feel fear that they'll never know comfort or see their loved ones again. I wonder which ones are grieving the way I am. I leave a liquor store, find an alley behind the shelter and hunker down beneath a fire escape. I'm not alone. There are six others in this crack between the apartment buildings: five men and one woman.

No one speaks to me. The first few hours are uneventful. I drink when no one is looking. The temperature drops and I get restless, dozing off and on. There are blue tarps tied above us, provided by some of the guys who sleep here regularly. One of the guys walks toward me. I'm frightened at first.

"Hey dude," he says, "if it starts to rain you can come over with us under my tarp."

"Oh thanks," I reply, feeling guilty as I register a fear within me.

Eventually one of the guys and the woman disappear. It looks like they're going to have sex.

I drift off, and then wake up to hear some of the men weeping. One of the men begins to shout a conversation to no one, something about a war.

One of the men starts singing: "I am going; I am going, where streams of whiskey are flowing. I am going; I am going any which way the wind may be blowing." I hum along. Ain't it the truth? I fall back into a deep sleep.

The next time I awake, bells are ringing out from the Catholic Church a few blocks down. Much to my dismay, a tall fence to keep the homeless from sleeping on the steps surrounds the church. I imagine that if Jesus were here right now, and if he was who the Holy Scriptures say he was, this is where he'd be, based on the little knowledge I have of him. This place is hell. At least it's what I imagine hell to be. The wind rips right through me and I laugh to myself at how inconsistent my thoughts are in relation to the character of God. Just an hour ago I was raging against a God who was a sadist, consciously tormenting me.

The city is full of wandering lost souls, driven mad by grief, addiction and regret. Their eyes are full of stories. There isn't much I wouldn't do for peace of mind and I realize they are no different. I'm riddled with guilt looking at these people. There isn't much I wouldn't do to help patch together the crying men in this alleyway. And then a truth dawns on me: I don't think of much else but myself. I imagine my pain and I are special, but the whole world is full of people like me. I wonder if there is anyone or anything capable of restoring all of us. I don't think there is, at least not in this life.

I'm staring hard at a dumpster thinking on that when I notice the words "forgive yourself" are spray-painted on the front of it. Why the hell did someone tag that on a dumpster? What are the chances I'd see it?

Something shatters in me and I pound my palms against my forehead. A part of me imagines Lenai leaving the words there for me, knowing someday I'd make my way to the alley looking for answers. But there's no place for forgiveness in my mind. There is no room for redemption. Even if there were some way to put myself back together, I wouldn't be keen on the idea. Why should I be happy and whole while Lenai is dead? It would be a betrayal.

I think that's where the impossibility of continuing to live stems from. It seems selfish that I recover from her death; I promised to love her forever. What does that mean if I just move on? I'm honest with myself about my plans for suicide. The hope is that I leave all this behind. The true dilemma is that I don't want to hurt anyone when I go. I'm terrified that I will leave Maraye in a pain deep enough to drive her into the world in this alley. If we grow closer and I go through with it and kill myself, it would be my indifference that sends her here. My anger grows with my thoughts. I don't want to love her, but I don't know how to stop.

I sit and think for a few more hours before I head for the subway. The airport is crowded. Families, couples and businessmen hurry through the terminal, never stopping to look at the people around them. It makes me question as I push my way through the terminal: how can a man be lonely with all these people in the world?

My flight is uneventful, save for the hour it rained. It was interesting to be in the midst of exploding clouds. Eventually we emerge from the rain and I doze on and off for the remainder of the flight.

Maraye is waiting for me at the terminal in Nashville. I see her standing nervously in the waiting area. She's shining in her sunflower dress and red flats.

"Did you get what you needed?" she asks quietly into my ear as we embrace.

"Yeah, I think so."

"Emmett, do you mind if we stop off somewhere on the way back?"

"Sure. Is everything alright?" I wonder where she wants to stop and why.

"Yeah, I just need to do something," she says simply.

We make our way to her car. I hate traffic and rush hour is miserable. It's nice talking with Maraye. I introduce her to punk bands and she plays Johnny Cash. We're finally out of the city when I realize we're heading the wrong direction on the freeway.

"Where are you going?" I ask, slightly annoyed.

She turns down the radio. "I don't want to go home today."

"What do you mean?"

"I just think we should get away," she says, staring ahead. I can't read her face.

"Wait ... Are you kidnapping me, Maraye?"

"That's one way to see it," she says with a slight smirk.

"You're insane, but okay," I laugh.

Her spontaneity makes me feel slightly forgetful when I realize I'm getting an extended break from the empty cabin. "Where are we going, Maraye?"

"The Smoky Mountains. We're going camping." She's excited and I can't help but smile despite my hesitation.

"What do you mean camping? You mean in tents and sleeping bags?" I ask incredulously.

"I mean you need to cowboy up and just come along for the ride," she says laughingly.

Eventually she pulls off and parks at a campsite. We're completely alone and the woods are silent.

"We have to hike a few miles," she tells me, handing me a bag and a pack full of supplies.

"Maraye, you're seriously insane."

I fall for her spontaneity, a helpless victim to her whims. This is a side of her I haven't seen until now. I like it.

The hike isn't bad. We're both in good shape and the terrain is mostly scenic and flat. It's autumn leaf season. The trees are a mixture of yellow birch, American beech, mountain maple, hobblebush, and pin cherry. When we get to a level knoll on the edge of a drop, Maraye decides to set up camp. It's a perfect overlook; the trees meld together like a brilliant mural despite the overcast weather.

Once we set up our tent and settle in, Maraye takes me on another hike to the Ramsey Cascades. The waterfall is at least a hundred feet high. We sit on a rocky outcrop a few hundred feet from the fall and stare out into the old growth and pool of water within it. It's the most beautiful thing I've seen since I arrived in Tennessee.

"Those are basswoods and silver bells," she says pointing into the hardwood.

"They're incredible," I tell her.

She looks sideways at me, starts to say something, stops herself and then starts up again. "Do you like it out here, Emmett?"

Without meaning to, I reply, "I like it a lot, especially with you here."

I glance over and see Maraye smiling back at me. The falls rage in front of us.

"I came here with my mom," she tells me, tapping a stick on her knee. "I don't miss her the way I did when I was younger, but I love her the same way I always have."

Her eyes reflect a soft remorse.

"I never knew my mother. She died from a kidney infection when I was young," I tell her.

"I'm sorry. I understand. Why don't you talk about your family? Don't they worry about you?"

"Nah, it was just my grandpa and I. We had a good run. I'm grateful for it. I'm on my own now," I answer, staring into the hardwood.

Maraye slides across the rock and sits next to me. Her legs are almost touching mine. I can nearly feel the warmth of her skin.

"Well, aren't we two peas in a pod?" she says, chuckling a little.

I laugh and smirk at her.

"Yeah, I guess we are."

We're mostly silent on the walk back to our campsite. Maraye starts a fire at the edge of the overlook.

"I only brought breakfast food," she tells me, laughing.

"That's perfect. I love breakfast."

We cook bacon and eggs out of a skillet over the fire. Her skin is lovely in the glow of the fire. Next to us I hear the scraping of bark as a lizard warms itself by the fire.

"It seems strange to me that someone might prefer a shopping mall to this," I say, making conversation. "I guess some people are subconsciously frightened of anything that might stir something aesthetic inside them."

"What do you mean?" she asks, flipping the bacon.

I pause for a moment, casually stirring the fire with a stick.

"I just think that, deep down, they're afraid to have to face their doubts and fears, so they avoid anything that makes them feel deeply. Those things could snowball before they know it. They might end up like me."

"What does that mean? What's wrong with you?" she asks, concern on her beautiful face.

"Not just me. I'm sure it happens to everyone eventually. Once you cross over into a certain plane of thought, you can't go back. You can't just live absentmindedly, ignoring the problems of being human, of being alive. It's a sad fate. At least it seems that way to me."

I feel bad for dragging Maraye into my mess of thoughts but it's nice to say these things out loud to a real person.

"Emmett, you have a knack for getting me to think about the things I don't like to think about. You don't think you can reconcile with your new thoughts?"

"I haven't been able to so far. I can hardly sustain the will to live, much less reconcile everything that's been stolen from me," I admit.

"What do you mean 'sustain the will to live?' You're all right, aren't you? I mean I know you're trying to figure some things out, but you're ok, right?"

She sounds panicked now, which is exactly what I wanted to avoid.

"I don't want to talk about it. I'll be fine," I lie.

"That scares me, Emmett," she replies, staring straight into my face.

"I'm fine. I promise." I try to look like I'm concentrating on the fire. I'm not sure that I come off as convincing.

She bites her lip and looks upward, staring into the night sky.

"Maraye, do you want to know a secret?"

"Of course. Is it your secret?"

"Yes," I say, slightly surprised by her question.

"Tell me," she says expectantly.

"I adore the way you bite your lip."

My confession is worth the embarrassment when Maraye anxiously covers her mouth with her hand. She laughs loudly and chucks a stick at me.

"Dammit, Emmett! Now I'm self-conscious," she says with softness on her face. She is laughing but she is absorbing the fact that my confession means I see her. She looks at me, something different in her eyes.

The fear that I'll send Maraye into suffering chokes me out as I look back at her. I'm not sure where to go from here, so I don't speak. I turn to look into the trees. The wind carries the smell of rosemary and some kind of wood that smells like a cheap cigar. It presses the grass against my feet. My thoughts turn to Maraye's skin once again. She catches me staring at her legs and pulls them to her chest, hiding a smile.

"Maraye, what do you want out of life?" I ask.

She blushes a bit and fights the urge to bite her lip once more.

"I want to dance and garden. I just want to have a simple life, I think. It would be nice to dance and sing and be in love."

"Dance? Like a ballerina?" I ask, smiling.

"No, not necessarily. I've danced since I was real young … you know, in school plays and community productions. I stopped not too long after I started dating Kevin. He told me it was a waste of time. He came with one of his friends to watch me perform in a play about Amelia Earhart once. I heard them laughing and I stopped dancing after that."

I shake my head in disbelief. "That guy's a prick. Maraye, I'd love to watch you sing and dance. You shouldn't let anything deter you from doing what you love."

"Why not? Didn't Lenai do that to you?" she asks, a bit of impatience in her voice.

"That's different. I …"

Before I can compose myself Maraye cuts me off.

"Jesus, Emmett… I'm sorry, that was out of line."

"No, it's alright," I say, shrugging. "I just think you deserve to be happy."

"Thanks," she mumbles.

We sit in silence for a bit, poking the fire and throwing stones into the flames. After a while Maraye gets up and crosses the fire, lying next to me.

"Tell me more about the stars," she says, moving so close that I feel her arm pressed against mine. The sensation this produces is an exciting sort of fear that fills my head, making the blood flow into my cheeks that I'm grateful she can't see in the dark. She makes me tremble despite the threat of Lenai's memory creeping in, spreading guilt through every cell of my body.

"Well," I start, pointing to the sky. "The summer triangle is nice in August; Vega, Deneb and Altair form a triangle above the Milky Way. There's an Asian myth that tells the story of two lovers separated by an angry Goddess. They say she scratched a river, hence the Milky Way in the sky to separate the two lovers, Vega and Altair. But I don't think that angry goddesses separate lovers. Death does that. Death, time and distance."

I sound like a bitter child.

"Why should love stop at death, Emmett? Isn't there a love as strong as death? Maybe you can choose to love? I don't think any force on earth can take that choice from you," Maraye says, stubbornness in her voice.

"Maybe," I say, not convinced in the slightest. "Aren't you afraid of anything? Aren't you afraid of God, or life, or death?"

I feel her gaze shift from the night sky to me. I turn to meet her eyes.

"I'm afraid of many things, I guess," she admits. I'm afraid that I'll never be loved. I'm afraid of being alone. Until you showed up I was alone. It was just my grandpa and me. I was scared I'd always be alone in this town."

"Has that fear always been in you or did it start with that guy?" I ask.

"Kevin. His name was Kevin. Yes, I think it got stronger because of him. What are you afraid of, Emmett?"

She inches closer, her shoulder pressing against mine. I hope she doesn't notice the way I shake when her skin grazes mine. Her pale white skin glows in the light of the fire.

"Me? I'm afraid that if God does exist, if there is a creator, he's just as confused about life and death and love as I am. Mostly I'm afraid that I'll continue to exist after I die."

"Why are you afraid of that?"

I'm silent for a moment. I collect my thoughts and wait for the desperation to recede.

"If I do continue to exist, if my reality and perception continues on in some other plane, it means that everything happening here means something. I'm worried I won't figure out what it all means in time. Sometimes I feel like I'm doomed to screw it up and be punished for it. Maybe I'm already being punished." I can hear the emotion in my own voice, making it a shade huskier. I wonder if Maraye notices.

"Well maybe we're just supposed to love with all we are, while we can. That seems like a purpose that could sustain a life. I think it's human to search for a meaning to life. Isn't loving as good a meaning as any?" she asks, her eyes serious.

"Maybe, but I think whatever I am that loved is ruined," I confess. "Maybe that's why I'm in this mess."

"I think if there's a force that can ruin you Emmett, there must be a force that can put you back together."

I turn my gaze to the stars and wonder to myself it there's anything like that for mankind. Could it be that simple?

"You know what else I'm afraid of, Maraye?"

"What?"

"I'm afraid you'll let some jackass destroy your self-esteem and confidence. I'm worried that you've stopped aspiring because of Kevin."

"You aren't the only one," she whispers.

In the dark as Maraye sleeps, I think of Lenai. I fight with myself about my feelings for Maraye most of the night. Eventually the wishful dreams win out and I allow myself to imagine a life with her as I drift toward sleep. I imagine what it would be like to recover from my grief and give myself to Maraye. But an unusual feeling spreads through me. I roll to my side and weep silently, imagining that Lenai is watching me from some place and hurting because of my betrayal. I watch Maraye as sleep begins to overcome me. The conflicting desire, fear and guilt make my stomach ache.

The sun is bright and the ground, damp. I'm perched on a log trying desperately to construct a decent breakfast for Maraye.

"You don't have to do this Emmett. I can cook."

"Nonsense, it's my turn to cook for you," I say, looking at her out of the corner of my eye. She is beautiful in the morning light.

I serve her the food I've prepared and I laugh as I watch her try to stomach the burnt bacon.

"At least you didn't burn the eggs," she says cheerfully.

"I'm sorry," I tell her between my laughter. "I overestimated my ability to be a competent outdoorsman."

"It's fine. You're a sweetheart for trying. No one's ever cooked for me before."

When we finish eating, we clean up and head to the falls again. Maraye has a grin on her face the entire hike but I'm not sure why until we reach the falls.

"Come on Emmett! Let's live a little!" she shouts over the roar of the water.

"There is no way in hell I'm getting in that water," I shout back.

"Do it for me! Please?"

"No, Maraye! No way!"

My main objection is not the cold but the idea of her seeing me in my briefs. I'm rendered a self-conscious child. More terrifying than that is the thought of her seeing me in my briefs as I look upon her in her underwear. I'm only a man after all. I can't be held responsible for my body's response to a gorgeous, half-naked woman. In the end I have no choice. She's very persistent.

I convince her to turn around while I undress and get in the water. In the sunlight her skin is shining as she undresses. I look away quickly but I catch a glimpse of her collarbone and breasts beneath her bra. She catches my gaze and the look she gives me speaks without sound. She sticks out her tongue playfully and hops into the water, shouting all the way.

"I'm going to regret this! Shit!" I shout, following her into the frigid water.

More than anything I want to wrap my hands around her ribs and pull her to me. Her unblemished, alabaster body is visible in the water. Her beauty outshines even that of the falls around us. My desire fills and fills. I didn't think I would feel like this again. In the back of my head I recall the last time I gave in to the whims of my lust. I push the thought away.

I'm completely defenseless to her playful splashing and teasing as she spits water in my face. It's a wonder I can move at all when she jumps on my back, laughing and squealing, as I grab hold and dunk her behind me. Things get tense as we tread water face to face. I forget to breathe as she whispers to me, "If this isn't nice, I don't know what is."

For a moment I think she's going to press her lips against mine but she only pushes down on my head, trying to hold me under.

This is the first day I've felt truly happy since Lenai died.

My happiness is so intense that it refuses to succumb to my usual self-condemnation. Today we're just two kids searching for something, something we've found in each other. She stays next to me as we dive to the bottom of the pool and back again. I emerge almost feeling born again. The pain is more distant than ever before.

"Emmett, I like seeing you smile."

I feel my smile fade as the guilt seeps into my brain. I tell myself that I can't betray a dead girl but the feeling continues to amplify. Maraye looks at me full of knowing. She purses her lips and narrows her eyes.

"Come back, Emmett," she says softly as she treads near me. "Where do you go when your eyes go blank? Are you with her?"

She's pained and worried. I don't know what to say to her. It strikes me that she effortlessly forces me to be honest, all of the time.

"I go back where I came from, 'cross the Milky Way."

"Oh, well I wish you'd stay with me," she says, her body moving closer to mine.

"I am with you. I'm right here," I say. Without meaning to, I move away from her in the water.

"No you aren't. You're far away."

She dives back down beneath me.

I'm not sure how to be her friend, much less her lover, but I want to be both right now. I purse my lips and look around at the swirl of hemlock, magnolia and sycamore surrounding me. A soft breeze sets fire to the cold.

I'm not sure if it's Maraye, my sobriety, or both but something has heightened my senses. The cattails on the bank bend ever so slightly in the weak wind. I smell the honeysuckle each time we emerge from baptizing ourselves over and over in the effort to dive deeper.

Maraye and I shiver and shake our way back to the warmth of our camp. We change and dry out. For a short while we sit together in silence, looking out at the view in front of us. The hills dip and cut through the landscape. The sound of the fire igniting brings me back from my thoughts and Maraye sits down next to me.

We eat peanut butter and jelly sandwiches before wrapping ourselves in our sleeping bags. We still haven't recovered from the cold of the falls. I don't notice that she is unconscious until I hear her soft snores next to me. I'm fond of this idiosyncrasy. She sleeps close to me without stirring. I think to myself that I'll never know that kind of sleep again. I stare up at the sky, feeling forever separated from my love.

Dozing off I think to myself, "Where are you, Lenai?" as I sink into a dreamless sleep.

In the morning it hits me as we pack up camp: familiar, overwhelming guilt moving over me and attaching itself to my mind. It's the same guilt that I felt two nights ago, but stronger now. I nearly panic from the weight of it. My chest is tight and I refuse eye contact with Maraye. I'm torn between sorrow for her and a feeling of betrayal for Lenai. It grows and grows as we hike back to the car and head back to Paris. All I can think about is getting rip-roaring drunk and forgetting the way that I feel about all this.

CHAPTER 5

This morning I got overly drunk and vomited several times. I've been consistently drunk since I returned from the falls. I can't shake the guilt and feeling of betrayal that's been hovering over me. I've had a hard time sleeping so I've switched from American Honey to a regimen of Jaeger and energy drinks. Even without the dreams, Lenai dwells in all my thoughts. I drink for every hour I lose sleep.

It takes a few hours of contemplative sleeplessness before I realize I'm drinking myself to death. I decide to leave even though it's the middle of the night. I want to take a drive and see where I end up. There are probably better ways to stay sober but I like the open road. I make sure to leave a note for Maraye and Jack on my front door letting them know I'll be back soon so they don't worry. It's a self-imposed exile; I'm afraid to spend more time with Maraye. I can't handle the weight of the guilt except by drinking, but I know I have to figure out another way to survive.

I head west down I-70 thinking of places to visit before my time runs out. I stop off in St. Louis and take a tram up the top of the Arch. It's more of a cube than a tram and I get slightly claustrophobic. Beyond a nice view and my admiration of human innovation I'm relatively unimpressed with St. Louis and decide to move on after an hour or so.

When I get to Denver I decide to get a hotel for the night. A war breaks out in my mind, fueled by worry. I don't like the idea of being away from Maraye and I'm angry when the worry wins out. I try to rationalize, telling myself that she might need me for something. I make up my mind to head back to Tennessee in the morning.

Despite the miniature God and Devil raging inside my head I somehow manage to appreciate the sight of the mountains and the fresh air. I break open my copy of Tolstoy's *Confession* and dig in, occasionally stopping to stare at the Rockies in front of me. Much of my own despair is mirrored in Tolstoy's writings. He writes:

Today or tomorrow sickness and death will come (they had come already) to those I love or to me; nothing will remain but stench and worms. Sooner or later my affairs, whatever they may be, will be forgotten, and I shall not exist. Then why go on making any effort? How can man fail to see this? And how go on living? That is what is surprising! One can only live while one is intoxicated with life; as soon as one is sober it is impossible not to see that it is all a mere fraud and a stupid fraud! That is precisely what it is: there is nothing either amusing or witty about it, it is simply cruel and stupid.

His remedy was faith in God. I can't help but confess to myself that the author of creation must be very lovely to have created mountains, oceans and forests. My ever-shifting view of whether "God" does or doesn't exist does not feel like something that can ever be resolved in me.

I imagine Tolstoy felt the same way when he considered faith while sitting in some distant forest. Tolstoy wrote that he was reborn in a forest. I wish I could hope that the same thing would happen to me. It's just not that simple, though. What good is life at all if you consistently have to start anew in order to avoid the kind of hopelessness I'm feeling? If trees had a consciousness I imagine they'd be asking the same questions, their leaves blooming and dying year in and year out.

The futility of youthful dreams constantly fading and blurring is enough to drive a person mad. The parents and teachers who say that you can achieve your dreams fail to mention that it makes no difference whether or not you achieve anything. Everything just fades away. Everyone just leaves or dies.

The sounds of the passing trucks remind me of the summer before college when I aimlessly roamed the country, hitchhiking and train-hopping. I miss my backpack. I miss the sensation of removing noisy headphones only to feel the stark silence of the empty open desert around me. I often took to city streets at night where there was always the same kind of people out and about; searching for fixes or hands to hold. They were just trying to stop being so damn lonely.

If I'm completely honest I prefer to be away from human beings for the most part. I don't like what we're doing to this planet and I don't like the things people do to each other. Imagine the goodness of a man just shrugging his shoulders and being good to the people around him. No more judgments about a person's beliefs, appearance or sexual orientation. There are times when I believe that people can live that way, but when I see that people are willing to kill, hate and reject strangers because of what they've read in old magic books, I'm not so sure.

I've never experienced anyone else's faith as providing sufficient answers to my questions and it never bothered me until now. I suppose if I try, I can choose to believe that having a certain set of beliefs will enhance my life, but deep down I know that's just bullshit. Religious nut jobs scream and hammer at people to adhere to their ideas. They're just afraid of their safety net being dismantled. They don't want to lose their shelter from the storm. I can't blame them but I'm unable to join them. This morning I find myself having a more favorable view of God, but I can't even say exactly why.

"I have these beliefs," they say on Sunday, "and these beliefs make me feel better about life. These beliefs help me make sense of things where there is no sense to be found."

But the truth is that any fool can apply meaning to this or that, or add meaning to this or that experience in their life. It's a game of psychosomatic coping. Jesus never gave any of his followers any answers, so why they hell do his followers claim to have them? When did he never explain the meaning of life or the purpose of humanity?

The only religious instruction that I've ever received was as a child when my grandpa would take me to church with him. I'd sit in Sunday school and listen to the tales of murder, rape and betrayal. I was told that God would fix my loneliness and make me content. I was told that God would make me happy. I trusted these things when I was a child, but as I grew older and became more studied, finding faith in God was like trying to catch smoke with my fingers. All of these thoughts and questions are getting old. The promised comfort of religion or faith has eluded me despite the claims of past religious instructors.

I work my way through a cup of coffee on the balcony of my room. The mountaintops paint the landscape in front of me. Their tops are stained with gray and white. My grandpa and I came here when I was much younger to float down the Royal Gorge. It's hard to imagine how much time has passed since those days. My thoughts about God and the past lead nowhere so I grab my pack and check out.

Near the Kansas border my thoughts turn to Maraye. It worries me that I miss her the way I do, despite hardly knowing her. It'll be a miracle if she continues to tolerate my coming and going whenever I please.

One day I might leave Paris and never return, especially if Maraye continues to chip away at my self-condemnation. I intended for Paris to be a place of penitence for me. Besides, I know that a woman cannot provide lasting contentment. She cannot cure my anguish, but she does alleviate it. I won't rely on her the way I've come to rely on alcohol when I become overwhelmed. It would be a disservice to her if I put that kind of pressure on her. It would be dishonest of me to consider a distraction a solution.

My thoughts on Maraye are interrupted when I glance down and see Lenai's picture tucked below the speedometer. The pain surfaces and I'm tempted to smash my head on the steering wheel. She should be sitting next to me. We should be young, happy and free. I shouldn't be a drunken idiot aimlessly living to die and I should not have such inconsistent and unsteady thoughts.

I'm nearly to the point of collapse when I stop to eat at a truck stop. I make my way through the grizzled truckers and traveling yuppies and retreat to a corner in the café. After I order my food an older man takes up a seat at the table next to mine, smiling at me as he sits. There's no one with him. He's wearing a mustard yellow shirt and plaid tie. A large gold band is wrapped around his ring finger. He notices my gaze and smiles once more.

"You're too young to be traveling alone," he says.

His nose hairs make my reply a bit stilted.

"I'm seasoned," I say, smiling politely, but truly wishing that he would leave me alone.

"Where ya headed? Back home to a sweetheart?" he drawls, raising his eyebrows knowingly.

The irony of his question hits home and I'm tempted to laugh.

"Nah, no sweetheart. I'm just wandering, I guess."

"I see," he smiles, "but not all who wander are lost. You're young. Enjoy it while you can."

"I'll try to remember that."

He doesn't take the hint and continues talking.

"My sweetheart is six feet under," he tells me, his words seemingly pain-free. "We never had any children, but we were lucky to have thirty-six wonderful years together. When you find a sweetheart, you hang onto her as long as you can."

"I will," I say, turning my head to show I'm not wanting to continue the conversation.

Men like this sadden me. His wife has become a plot in the ground that he talks to at times. I promised myself that I'd never reduce Lenai to a hole in the ground. I told myself that I'd never reduce her to a headstone with some words etched in it. My love for Lenai is no different than his love for his wife. I guess everyone attempts to feel the ones they've lost in different ways. People aren't all that different after all.

He sips his coffee while looking around the restaurant. I can't help but wonder if he conjures delusions of his dead love. We're all destined for the same sorry state. Maybe Lenai was the lucky one. I hate myself for thinking this thought. How I'm paying for her peace.

I know just by looking at this man that he's lonely and looking for companionship. I understand the desire to find a crowd at times. He's probably a local. It wrenches my insides and I know I'd rather die now than carry on until I'm as despondent as he is, sitting alone in a truck stop café. After I eat I leave the café behind me. I don't want to know how his story ends, although I imagine it ends like all stories end. All rivers flow to the ocean, after all.

Occasionally I stop off at a rest stop to stretch my legs and smoke a cigarette. I'm in no hurry and I want to appreciate the scenery. It will likely be the last time I see it. The peaks of rock and dirt stab into the air. The more I meditate on the past and the future, the closer I come to suicide. It feels like I'm losing the battle to sustain myself. My thoughts are becoming more hopeless with each day that passes. If I'm smart I'll end myself before Maraye becomes too attached or vice versa.

A train sounds in the distance and I watch as a family snaps pictures of themselves overlooking the canyon behind me. Someday they'll likely be scattered and separated by circumstances they can't foresee. But they're happy and whole now, smiling and laughing in the cold. Spirals of white begin to drift slowly from the gray sky as I drive off. I need to clear my head.

On one hand I know others would say that it's sad to see the world the way I am seeing it, but from where I stand it is the most honest way. The truth becomes clear when you spend your nights cold and alone. The truth is veiled when you spend your nights with someone warm and moving. Life lived next to someone else tricks you into holding onto silly sentiments like hope and redemption. It's impossible to know what's good or bad and only cowards are afraid to admit it. Tragedy tips the scale toward bad and it's next to impossible to see the world in any other way after that. Even familiar, comforting distractions begin to lose their flavor.

My mournful reverie is interrupted when my phone rings. I don't recognize the number but I answer anyway.

"Hello?"

"Emmett? Is that you?"

"Yeah, it's me. Maraye?"

"Oh good. Yeah, it's me. I'm sorry for bothering you."

"That's alright. What's going on?"

"I'm sorry. I just had a bad dream and I wanted to talk to you. Is that okay?"

The sound of her voice in the receiver is soft and sweet. Her voice is hoarse and high-pitched, suggesting that she's still half asleep. It makes me beam.

"Oh, yeah, that's all right. I'm driving back to you. I mean I'm driving back to Paris."

She laughs, catching my slip-up, and I feel the blood in my face warm my cheeks.

"Are you safe, Emmett? I had a terrible nightmare that something happened to you," she says, her voice sounding a little bit more awake now.

"Yeah, I'm okay, I promise. Are you alright?"

"I'm okay. I was just worried about you. Did you find what you're looking for?"

"No. I saw some mountains though. They were nice," I say. I imagine the way she looks right now.

"Oh, I've always wanted to go west and see the mountains. I've never been west," she says wistfully, yawning.

"It's beautiful. Maybe I'll take you someday," I reply without thinking.

"Really?"

She's excited at the prospect and I feel like a damn fool. I didn't intend to say that. I know that I won't be alive long enough to live that with her. I'm letting this get out of hand but I decide to lie.

"Yeah, it would be fun."

I feel the collision of the reality of Maraye and Lenai's ghost within me. Lenai's memory is so real in moments, but Maraye's voice interrupts those memories and beckons me onward.

We talk for hours. Her voice makes the dreary haul through Kansas a blur. Somehow she manages to make me laugh and before I know it I'm crossing the Tennessee border through Missouri without remembering much of the drive. All the while Lenai is ever present in my subconscious. My feelings for Lenai are still there, buried beneath my new distraction. I try not to focus on them so they don't overcome me, but I still feel sick and I am not able to be fully happy.

"Emmett? Can I see you tonight? If you're not too tired? I just want to know you're all right."

I want to deny her but I can't find it in me. I want to be near her. Her gentleness is compelling and demanding. The force of

Lenai's memory and Maraye's presence threatens to tear me in two. It takes all of my strength not to succumb to my anguish. Despite my hesitation I push down on the accelerator and rush back to Paris.

I think of the days we spent camping together in the mountains. I think of how I kept my distance when I returned by avoiding her. I can't think of any option that won't be cruel to Maraye in some way. I realize that my only option may be to choose the lesser cruelty.

My thoughts shift from problem solving to the way her legs felt as they pressed against mine as we sat together at the falls. What am I doing?

When I finally pull into the drive way I see Maraye standing down at the marina, looking at the lake.

"You're here," she says, hearing my footsteps approaching. She beams at me and I'm surprised again by her beauty.

"I am," I say, smiling back at her.

She runs right into my chest, nearly knocking the wind out of me, as she wraps her arms around me. I feel her hands gently tug at my sweater as she buries her head in my neck. I freeze.

"I'm glad you're alright. I was worried that you'd gone away for good."

My hands lie awkwardly to my side. I begin to reach for her but I falter and pull them back. I feel the familiar guilt as I half-heartedly return her embrace. The desire for her is present but I have no intention of sharing any kind of physical intimacy with anyone who isn't Lenai.

"I'm sorry, Maraye," I say, not sure of how to explain what I'm feeling.

"For what?"

"For scaring you," I answer. It's true; I am sorry I scared her, but I'm sorry for so many other things that I don't know how to put into words.

"Sit with me," she says, motioning toward the end of marina.

We sit next to one another, our feet dangling a few inches above the water. I have to fight off my arachnophobia when I notice about a dozen Dolomede spiders sitting in their webs, attached to the marina only inches from our bodies.

"They're harmless," Maraye says, noticing my discomfort. "They freak me out, too, though."

I laugh nervously.

"I never noticed them before. I can't believe I've been so close to them this whole time."

I feel her sigh next to me and glance over to see a half smile on her face. She seems afraid to speak but she carries on anyway.

"You've been avoiding me," she says bluntly.

"Yes. I have. I'm sorry."

"It's okay. You don't need to explain. I think I understand. I'm just really glad you came back."

She hesitates to look at me and stares out at the lake. I take notice of her legs dangling above the water. The moon illuminates their smooth, creamy texture.

"Maraye, I'm not used to any one worrying about me. I mean, not these days."

I'd like to give her a panoramic view of my past and where I'm heading, so that she can really understand who I am in this moment, but I'm weary of constantly thinking about myself and I wonder if she is, too. I'm beginning to despise myself for that.

"I didn't mean to frighten you, Maraye. I just have a hard time sitting still. Sometimes I just need to get out and feel free," I explain. That's a half-truth.

"You don't feel free here?"

"I do, but it's a different sort of freedom. Sometimes I just need to go where the road takes me. But I do like it here. It's dark enough to see the stars. It's not like that in New York. It's very conducive for a contemplative atmosphere."

I try to finish without laughing but fail.

"I'm a dumbass. I'm sorry."

"No you aren't. Do you think you can think your way out of this mess?"

Her question takes me by surprise.

"What do you mean?"

"I just mean life. Do you think you can figure life out?" she asks, looking at me searchingly. I look away.

"I don't know. I'm afraid. And I'm tired of being afraid of life and death. I'm tired of everything. I'm tired of trying not to think about anything. I'm tired of my own thoughts, if that makes sense."

I turn my head to find her staring at me. She smiles gently and bites her lip, which makes me chuckle.

"You're doing it, Maraye."

"I know. I can't help it with you."

I wait for her to speak again, unsure of how to respond. She pauses for a moment as if she's collecting her thoughts and carries on.

"Life has really torn you to pieces, hasn't it?"

"Shit ..." I say, shaking my head as I think about the reality of my life.

Maraye is laughing with me and for a moment it feels like she really sees me. It's a heavy laughter. It feels almost holy on the silent lake.

"Okay, I admit that was a stupid question, but has it gotten better at all? Is the pain any easier now than it was when it was fresh?" she asks, looking at me apologetically. I can see that she's probing to find out just how screwed up and damaged I am.

"Some days it feels better than it did before. When it first happened it was a constant ache, even in sleep. Now it comes in waves. It will hit, then recede, hit once more, and then recede again. But I still see her. I mean I see her in my head. Sometimes I pretend that she's alive and safe with me. I see her walking toward me lit up like a seraph under the streetlights. I still feel the way my insides burned away when her mother called me with the news. I still think of the future that I'll never live out, all of our plans gone forever. Some nights I wish I could take the memories and throw them in the lake. I wish I could wave goodbye and slip into forgetfulness. I wish I could forget for good. I wish it weren't all such a mystery. I wish life didn't terrify me."

When I finish I cover my face and breathe in, feeling childish after my outburst. I didn't mean to say so much.

"It's funny to hear myself say all that out loud. I'm sorry, Maraye."

"Jesus Christ, Emmett, you don't ever need to be sorry. I can't even imagine, but I hope I'm with you when you figure a way out of this thing — —whatever it is."

"What's the point? Even if I find a way out of this I'll have to endure it again unless I'm lucky and die before the next time someone gets taken from me."

"Emmett! You don't know that. There's goodness in life. I know there is. You've brought goodness to my life."

She stops and then looks embarrassed.

"I'm sorry, Maraye, but my optimism just ain't what it used to be. It fades more and more every day. The truth is that I don't want to pull it all together just to see it fall apart again. It terrifies me. What's the point?"

"We all have to come back from the dead at some point, Emmett. That's just life, isn't it?" she says, her eyes serious.

"You sound like my grandpa. He used to say to me, 'Emmett, everyone who lives and loves is a phoenix.' I would nod my head then, but now I think that if that's life, it's a cruel fate."

"Maybe that's part of the test, choosing to love despite the inevitable suffering that accompanies it?"

I shake my head. "If life is a test, it's been rigged. It's a no-win situation. Who's testing us any way?"

"I don't believe in no-win situations, Emmett."

I don't know if she's quoting Captain Kirk but I laugh hard regardless. I briefly remember back to my admiration of Spock and his flawless logic.

"Maraye, did you mean to quote Captain..."

She cuts me off, wearing a devilish grin.

"I know my Star Trek, Emmett."

Once again our holy laughter echoes across the lake and I speak without thinking.

"Quoting Kirk makes you really attractive to a geek like me."

My accidental words cause her to turn crimson. The contrition floods through me and I stare down at the surface of the lake. It strikes me that Maraye and I have such an effortless rapport.

In another life ... I think to myself.

"Emmett, what do you think about Jesus?"

"Oh lord, I don't know. Where did that come from?" I ask fearfully.

I'm never inclined to discuss religion.

"I don't know. I just think it would be nice if there were a God who could make things new. You know, fix and restore people like you, like us, damaged goods and all."

"That would be nice." I say doubtfully.

"You don't think it's possible that he could put you back together?" she asks, her tone deadly serious.

I stifle my laugh, not wanting to offend her. I compose myself by biting my lip and twiddling my thumbs over it.

"I don't know. I've never met the guy. It seems like he was a nice fellow. The world would be a nicer place if Christians took him seriously."

"You don't like Christians?" She asks, in a tone that suggests I've offended her.

"I'm sure most of them are good people. I've got my problems with them, especially the church as a whole, I guess. Christians as a group seem to generally lack in the area of book smarts, or at least it seems that way to me. The majority of them don't seem to care about having an honest, intellectually defensible faith." I pause and try to choose my words carefully, yet honestly.

"I also don't think it would go over very well if I read the Sermon on the Mount to most Christians either." I tell her, nervously avoiding eye contact.

"Aha! What's that have to do with anything?" she seems unfazed by my disdain for faith.

I pause and compose my thoughts. I don't want to get into this but I tread forward any way.

"It's like Willie said: the devil can cite scripture for his purpose. It made me angry when I was younger. But now I just let it be. They need their tribal gods to get by, I guess, and if they can't use logic to further their agendas, why not use God to scare people? I hate bullies, and the biggest bullies are religious officials."

"Yeah, that's true I guess, I hadn't really thought about that. But take away all the people and ideas and Jesus seems like a nice idea." She looks at me for a response, and I nod in agreement.

"Yeah, I think so." I say.

Maraye seems satisfied with my response and proceeds to pull herself closer to me. We lay on our backs looking up at the clouds through the cracks of the marina cover. After a few minutes, she breaks the silence.

"It's sad to be so young and desire to be made new, isn't it?" My voice has dropped to a more peaceful sounding timbre. Maraye has a way of disarming my cynicism.

"I don't think it's completely sad." She says. "It means you were capable of loving, at some point. You were capable of loving something, or someone, with everything in you. That's not encouraged these days. I mean thought-filled living — it's not standard issue among society. Is it?"

I fall silent at her words. I look at her, amazed by her perception.

"Oh, I'm sorry I'm going on like this, Emmett. Hey, why are you biting your lip?" she asks, with a suspicious look on her face.

Her words bring me back from my thoughts. I realize that I'm smirking, and biting down on my lip. I regain my composure and smile at her.

"I guess you're rubbing off on me. But seriously, this is a good conversation. We have good conversations." I explain. "And I think you're right. People do everything they can, these days, to avoid thinking about the cost of loving another person. That's another one of those things Jesus talked about that people aren't taking seriously, but I can see why it isn't encouraged. He practically told all of us to kill ourselves. I mean the things he said about loving everyone all of the time. I mean look what love did to me... look at me... for Christ's sake."

Maraye's head jerks up and she turns to look at me with a worried expression.

"I like looking at you," she tells me, unashamed. I do my best to hide how happy her words make me.

"The past doesn't need to define you," she says. "Well at least it doesn't need to destroy you. Don't say things like that. You aren't dead and you can't go anywhere. People need you. At least, I need you to be okay."

I need to stop this from happening. This is what's worried me all along. I feel the apprehension move to the front of my thoughts. I'm afraid of hurting Maraye, the same way that Lenai's death has hurt me. It seems irrational that I believe I could cause that kind of damage to someone I hardly know, but the trepidation remains nonetheless. She is falling for me, exactly what I most wanted her not to do.

"Maraye, you can't get attached to me like that. It's not safe."

I'm hoping my words will put a halt to the intimacy we've begun to share, but she moves closer to me, seemingly unfazed. I don't want her to get in the way of my plans.

"I'll take my chances," she says, meeting my eyes directly. "Besides, you've gotten attached to me. I can see it in the way you look at me."

I don't know what to say. She's right. I feel it pour in and now I'm really confused. I don't know how to dig my way out of this mess. I just sit silent and stare out over the water into the forest. The starless sky taunts me as I look up, despairing at the irony of life. What's more tragic, Lenai's death or the inevitability that I'll wreck Maraye's life before this game is over?

"If I were remotely decent, I'd leave now before I drag you into my suffering. I'm not doing very well, with life, or anything right now," I confess, tossing a broken chunk of wood into the water.

"Don't leave. Stay with me, please," she persists. "I'm an adult, Emmett. I know what I'm getting into with you. I know I'm taking a risk."

"Why are you so interested in me, Maraye? I can't figure that out. Why me?" I ask as I reach in my pocket and pull out a cigarette to calm my nerves.

"Give me one," she says, holding her hand out.

"You smoke?" I ask incredulously, holding a lighter up for her, as she leans down toward the flame.

"Only sometimes," she tells me.

"And back to your question... It's because you're sweet, Emmett, and you're good. I can see that you're good. I just feel safe around you. I don't feel that way around anyone but you. You make me feel good about myself. I haven't felt that in a long time."

I grit my teeth and drive my nails into the calloused wood beneath me. I don't want to be like that Kevin guy was to her.

"I feel that way around you, too. I didn't think I'd want to be around anyone again."

"Does it make you feel guilty?" she asks, hesitantly. Her tone suggests that she already knows the answer to her question. She pushes her hair behind her ear, avoiding eye contact. Behind us, I hear a moth. Judging by the continuous thudding sound, it's repeatedly colliding with the hanging corridor light.

"Yes," I respond truthfully. "It's a burning and a guilt that never ends."

"I thought so, especially when we were at the falls. But you are happy when we're together, aren't you?"

Maraye rubs her arm for warmth. Her face lights up as I remove my hoodie and wrap it gently around her shoulders. A smile lingers on her face.

"Yes, I am happy when we're together," I tell her, "but I feel guilt as well."

"Oh," she mutters, in a disappointed tone. "Emmett, can I ask you something? I don't want you to get mad."

"Sure," I reply, stubbing my cigarette butt out. "I won't get mad."

"Okay," she says, breathing deeply. "Am I like her?"

"Like who?" I ask, placing my cigarette into an empty beer can, beside me.

"Am I like Lenai?"

Her question is one I'd like to avoid, but it doesn't anger me. At first I consider lying, but I reject the notion and pause for a moment. I want to choose my words wisely.

"Yes, I think so, in some ways. You make me feel young when I'm with you. She always told me that I was trying to be old too quickly. But Maraye —whenever I'm with you — I'm with you." I do my best to sound firm, and make eye contact. I want her to know that I'm serious.

"You are?" she asks, looking satisfied.

"Yes, I am. I'm normally very conscious of things like that. I'm with you because you're you. And I like you."

She lights up at my words and nudges my shoulder with the side of head. I give up resisting for the night. I'm completely with Maraye, for now.

"That makes me glad," she says. I hear a slight sizzle as she drops her cigarette into the beer can. "I won't press it again. I just want to be me, you know? Not someone else and not a replacement."

"Okay, can I ask you a question?" I ask, taking my turn.

"Yes, of course." She responds casually.

"Did you love Kevin?"

At first I think I've made her angry, because she's silent for a few moments. I think of apologizing, but she speaks.

"No, I never felt any love for him," she tells me casually.

"Never mind, we don't need to talk about that," I say, regretfully.

"It's all right. I want you to know my story, too. The truth is it was nice at first. I liked him but that wore off after a while. I just stayed with him because it seemed like it was what girls were supposed to do. Eventually, he got angry and controlling. He insulted me a lot and he hit me a few times when we fought. After that, fear mostly kept me with him. It took me a while to stop being afraid and weak. He wasn't gentle like you. He knew how to manipulate me and keep me controlled. When I confessed the situation to my grandpa he was pissed. He got me out of there in a hurry."

When she finishes she looks over at me. The look on her face tells me that she must feel pretty screwed up. Either that, or she's ashamed, or both. I think she's afraid of how I'll respond.

"It's strange," she tells me. "You're kind of like a calm chaos to me. Sometimes the things you talk about make my head a mess, but you have this way of staying composed, even when I can tell you're angry. I'm never afraid of you. I'm afraid of almost every guy I know, but not you."

She stops talking and pulls her knees up to her chin to rest her head.

"I'm never angry at you. I would never hurt you, Maraye."

She stretches her legs back out over the water. I take notice of her exposed thigh. My thoughts threaten to stray toward lust but I ignore them.

"I know you aren't angry at me," She tells me, her eyes filled with pity. "I wish you weren't angry at all. I'm sorry for you, Emmett. I know you probably hate that but I wish I could fix you."

"I don't need to be fixed," I say, somewhat bitterly. I don't like the idea of simply getting over Lenai.

"If you could only see yourself the way I do, Emmett," she whispers sweetly, pursing her lips.

I don't respond. We just sit in silence while I consider the way I feel about her. I tell myself that I can get out of this before I get too attached to her. Subconsciously, I don't want to think about it at all. I know I'm going to hurt her, but I'm too selfish to stop myself from doing what I'm doing. I'm leading her on and I can only hope that I'm not around to see Maraye suffer the way I am in the end.

The real irony is that what I'm doing to Maraye pushes me closer to suicide than ever, while at the same time, I worry that

I'll begin to think more of her than suicide. The disequilibrium of my thoughts is reaching a new level. I want to be drunk.

The distant humming of dragonflies draws my attention. I reach for the shot-size bottle of American Honey in my pocket, remove the cap and pour, reaching for the second bottle as I gulp. The suddenness of Maraye's voice shakes me and I nearly drop the bottle into the water.

"Why are you doing that? Did I do something wrong?" she asks, looking hurt.

"No, it's just the way I feel about you, and all of this. It's a lot to deal with. This isn't much." I say, shaking the tiny bottle. "It just helps quiet the noise in my head."

"Well it scares me." Her face is scrunched in disapproval.

"Yeah, but it's the only way I can stop thinking. It blurs things. You know?"

"I guess so," she says, unconvincingly. "But self-medicating is dangerous. It makes me worry about you."

"You can't worry about me," I reply, in an exasperated attempt at maintaining a healthy distance. I don't know why I'm still trying to keep my guard up.

My frustration starts to spill out and I kick the water below me. Her eyes widen and fill with moisture. For a moment, I think she's going to stand and leave.

"Maraye…" I say, apologetically. "I'm just so fucking scared. Fuck, I'm sorry. I don't mean to be like this."

It's a catch twenty-two. I need to be cruel and distant to keep her from getting attached. But I can't stand hurting her by acting that way. I can't hurt her. I don't have the willpower.

"It's okay," she tells me. "I knew you were feeling like this. It's just hard to hear it come out. I know you loved her, but there's still a lot of good in the world. We don't have to be romantic. We can just be here together, with each other, for each other. There are plenty of things to live for and be happy about."

I try to regain myself and restore my composure, but I continue to spew my thoughts on her.

"How can I live and be happy when I can't get my life back? It's not just Lenai I'm talking about either. I mean, whatever it is that causes us to persist, despite the utter futility of it all? I've lost that drive. If a person lives any length of time, they're going to have to endure the death of people they love. Most people get lucky and make it a few more years than I have before they lose it. People who say they're at peace before they die are probably just ready to get the hell away from all this suffering. I don't know what to do."

I end my rant and look over at Maraye. She tugs on the sleeve of my sweater and pulls my head into her shoulder. All I can do is hold my hands at my side and breathe. Her breath warms the side of my head as she whispers softly.

"I wish I could fix you, Emmett. I've never wanted to care about someone the way I want to care about you."

The sweetness and sincerity in her voice make me feel like I'm going to melt into the lake.

"You're here," I tell her. "That counts for something. And I'm still breathing. That counts for something, too." I mean it. She does make me feel a bit more peaceful, in spite of the guilt she inadvertently causes.

"What does that mean?" she asks.

"Never mind. I'm just tired," I lie, pulling myself away from her. She hasn't caught on that I'm suicidal and I need to keep it that way.

"Me, too. I'm exhausted. I have an idea," she tells me, with a grin.

"Oh yeah, what's that?"

"Let's watch a movie."

"What?" I ask, climbing to my feet.

She giggles and takes my hand as I pull her up. The gleam in her eyes ropes me in as she rises to her feet.

"I just want to watch a movie with you. You know that's what normal people do. I don't have to work tomorrow."

"Oh, I don't know." I say, picking up our cigarette can. "I'm kind of exhausted."

"Oh, come on, Emmett, watch a movie with me," she pleads. Her hands clasp together and she throws pouting eyes at me. She's got me right where she wants me.

"Okay, I guess it would be nice to do something normal," I say, defeated.

"Really?"

She looks excited. I can't help how I feel. And as much as it pains me, I'm overjoyed that I don't have to bid her farewell just yet.

"Hooray!" she yells at the top of her lungs. I just stare at her wide-eyed and laugh. I'm suddenly thrilled with the idea of relaxing with her.

We move slowly up to the house. The moisture from the wet grass soaks through my shoes and I glance over to see Maraye removing her tiny flats. She squeals and runs toward the cabin. "It's so cold, Emmett!"

I'm beginning to feel a bit overwhelmed. I'm afraid because I have no control. I desperately want to leave but I desperately want to be near her. I think to myself that none of this would have happened if I had put my silly questions aside and killed myself earlier. I'm too weak to continue living in this life knowing the grief that the future holds. I'm too weak not to glance at Maraye in her red dress. Goddamn her green eyes ...

When we take our places next to each other on the couch I see everything. Suddenly I'm aware of her shoulder blades and her porcelain skin under the straps of her dress. I notice the gleam from the television reflected on her legs. I see the way her bangs raise when she arches her eyebrow, grinning at me, when our eyes connect. She has me under her spell and she knows it. She doesn't hesitate before sliding in front of me. She lays horizontally, her figure framed perfectly in my sight.

The thing about this scene is that Maraye is not Lenai. Lenai is dead and I am lying here with another woman. It's an overwhelming kind of crushing that follows me as I stand, making for the bathroom. I shut the door behind me and brace myself as I collapse next to the sink. I stifle my sobs and ward off the urge to vomit. The guilt and anguish choke me out. I reach up and grab the towel hanging from the bathroom door, burying my face and cutting off the airflow. If there were a God, he'd strike me down as I lay here.

I think of Maraye. I fantasize about my fingers brushing through her hair, across her ribs and down her thighs but then my thoughts turn to Lenai. I remember her spine, her hips, and her knuckles. I remember that Lenai is dead and I am still here wishing to be in her place. My fist drives deep hard into the wall cracking the mushroom colored tile. I strike again and more tiles falls to the ground, this time slicing my knuckles.

I muffle my screams and wrap the towel in my hands around my fingers. I rest my head between the towel and toilet seat. Saline and saliva dampen the cloth as I sob uncontrollably. I am terrified of all the unending conflict in my mind. It's entirely overwhelming.

I fall silent when I hear Maraye speak from outside the door.

"Are you okay, Emmett? What was that noise?" she asks in a worried tone.

Somehow I manage to calm my shaking voice.

"I'm fine. I just knocked over the shampoo in the tub," I lie. I breathe into the towel.

"Oh, sorry!" she giggles. She's completely unaware.

"I'll be there in a moment." I cover my face and bite down on the towel.

"She promised …" I whisper to myself. "She promised she'd come back …"

After a few minutes I finally manage to stand and restrain my hysterics. Moving quietly I put the bathroom back in order. I splash hot water on my face, check myself in the mirror and head back to Maraye. We sit in silence for a while. She jumps several times as the movie plays.

"Why did I want to watch a scary movie about a cabin in the woods?" she asks, laughing after she nearly jumped off the couch.

Fatigue has finally caught up to me. I could sleep like an infant if I closed my eyes.

Maraye sits up beside me and looks at me with a concerned expression. "You're not okay, are you? Your eyes are a mess."

"Ain't this the bloodiest mess in the world?" I ask her, almost regressing to a state of hysteria again.

"It's a mess all right, Emmett," she says clutching my thumb with her finger. "You're going to be okay though."

"I really don't know. I think I'm dying, Maraye. I'm not alright." I'm just seconds away from losing control again. I'm a fucking mess.

"Well," she says placing her hand on my chest. "I'm here if that counts for anything."

"I think that might be the problem," I confess.

The words hurt me before they're even out. Tears roll down Maraye's face. I've never seen anything so perplexingly beautiful.

"I'm sorry this is happening to you. I'm so sorry I'm doing this to you," she says, wiping her face. "I can go. I'm so sorry," she says. She begins to stand but I grab her wrist.

"Wait," I blurt out. "I don't want to be alone right now. I'm sorry, Maraye. I'm just having a hard time. I haven't spent time with anyone, you know … not since Lenai. It hurts. It's confusing. I don't think I should be allowed to be happy like this."

She nods and places her hand on my cheek, cupping my face. For a moment the noise in my mind is silenced. I feel no pain at all as I wipe the moisture from her cheeks. Our faces move close together. Our lips tremble and twitch, our pulses race, and our bodies inch closer to one another.

"Maraye," I say dodging what feels like an inevitable kiss. "Thanks for being here with me." She smiles at me, releasing my face.

"It's going to be alright. Things will get easier," she says. Now watch this scary movie with me."

I smile as she curls up next to me, resting her head on my shoulder. We're fine for now.

"Maraye … I'm exhausted."

"Here …" she says, in a nurturing tone.

In the hallowed glow of the television and porch light she slides to the end of the couch and places her head on the armrest. I roll to my side and nervously place my body beside her. I stare out at the television. It's bright as the sun through my blurry vision and slowed thoughts. Involuntarily, my eyes close and I feel Maraye's hands run through my hair. The peace she brings wins out over my guilt.

There's only darkness.

CHAPTER 6

It's Sunday morning and I've reluctantly agreed to attend a church service with Maraye and Jack. As a man of science the prospect of attending church is horrifying enough, without it being a service in the Bible belt. I'm not inclined to listen to a man tell me the will of someone he's never met, but here I am. Truth be told, Maraye is the only reason I'm sitting in this pew. I'm a reluctant draftee.

She looks breathtaking as usual. Her legs are covered in moss green tights and a black skirt rests just above her knees. Her floral top reveals her collarbone and I track it down to her breasts before looking away. My thoughts are momentarily ablaze with lust. I cover my face to hide my smirk. I'm amused at my thoughts in a house of God.

Even Jack has swapped his overalls for a suit and tie. I'm feeling particularly self-conscious at the moment. Maraye has combed my hair and forced me to wear a tucked in shirt with a tie and cardigan. I look around and see that most of the congregants are older in age; several of them are staring at me. There are a few younger couples and several miserable looking children beside their parents. The church is small and in minor disrepair.

A stocky older man takes the pulpit, speaking in a booming voice. "God remembers the things we make ourselves forget. But he forgets the things we ask him to forgive."

A few people nod their heads at his words. I haven't the slightest clue what to make of what he's implying. After a short song sung by an older lady and her husband, the congregation stands and begins to recite the Pledge of Allegiance. I'm horrified, so I look over to see Maraye smirking at me. Is their God American? I don't think I can worship a capitalist.

They follow the Pledge of Allegiance with yet another song, this time sung all together, accompanied by the organ player. When they finish they recite another pledge. Their voices spill out like some kind of dissonant banshee choir gone hoarse and out of tune.

"I pledge allegiance to the Bible, God's Holy word, and will take it as a lamp unto my feet, a light unto my path, and hide its words in my heart that I may not sin against God."

I think it's some sort of bible pledge. A few of the congregants turn to stare at me as I sit silent and mortified.

"Maraye ..." I whisper. "Is this some sort of cult?"

"Just relax," she says in a whisper. "They think God really likes America." She cups her mouth to stifle her laughter.

I don't want to be here. If it weren't for Maraye I'd bolt for the door. I just stare downward at the pages as they make their way through hymns. Occasionally I'll glance up and catch a few somber faces staring at Maraye and me. They almost look envious in a way. It's strange to think of anyone envious of me, but most of them are here alone. That's the only explanation I have for their stares.

It strikes me that most of these folks are probably just contending with life and loss. My chest begins to ache for them. I stop seeing them as back-wood rednecks and townies. I see myself in their sad expressions. I am truly ashamed of my judgment. Many of them seem to be cracked and worn out like me. They look hollow, like remnants of who they once were. We're all that's left after the people we love were torn away. I can't help but wonder if they're here hoping God will put them back together. Ignoring all of the religious language, I try to decipher what this is really about. I think it's about loneliness.

I feel the true power from this ruined building and these ruined souls. I see their hope. At least I see people looking for hope. It's a powerful thing but I don't know that it can undo the despair I feel.

I suppose it doesn't matter much if their hope is misplaced. It helps some of them get by and that counts for something. Maybe it's helped Jack cope with the death of his wife and maybe it's helped Maraye cope with losing her mother. Maybe they expect it to save me from my anguish. I am sorry to disappoint them but it doesn't seem to have taken hold.

The pastor takes the pulpit when they finish singing the final hymn. It's hard for me to focus while he preaches. Surprisingly he avoids ranting against homosexuality, liberals, or Muslims. Admittedly most of my preconceived judgments have fallen flat. He mostly goes on about forgiveness and the joy of God. I don't buy it and I don't feel anything in response. I'm void of faith.

Does he think the pain and uncertainty is the devil inside? Did he lose a loved one and does he dream of meeting them again? Does Maraye sit here and hope to see her mother again? Does Jack come here to find hope that he'll be with his wife once more? Many of these things seem plausible. It's likely everyone here is seeking safety in one way or another. That seems very human to me.

We're all scared of what we'll find when we die. We're all scared of the mess we've made of this planet. I'm afraid that God will be out of forgiveness for fools like me. I don't mind coming here to work out what's before me. Maybe on a good Sunday souls really break out of their bodies. Maybe this place helps them be good to each other. It beats suffering in one place alone. I won't judge them for that.

Sadly, I don't think this place offers the solution I need to keep the razor from my vein. Trying to work this all out, staring at the stained glass windows, I imagine Sisyphus would have felt like, endlessly rolling that rock to the top of a mountain. It's during this thought that I pause to notice Maraye grinning at me. Everyone is standing again, singing some song. She nods for me to stand up, trying not to laugh.

When they finish the hymn the pastor offers up an altar call. He speaks for a while. I mostly blur it out and continue thinking. My thoughts are interrupted when I look up once again and find the congregants gazing at me. The pastor again repeats the call for lost souls to repent and accept salvation. When no one responds he leads us in a sinner's prayer. I feign reciting it and return to my contemplation. I'm not sure I have anything worth saving to begin with; it doesn't feel like there's much left.

Camus wrote that *crushing truths perish from being acknowledged*, and that *our fates belong to us*. I wish I could believe what he wrote. I wish it comforted me while I search for whatever it is I'm searching for but the crushing truths seem to persist in crushing me relentlessly. Regardless I hope these congregants carry the peace that their faith offers for the rest of their days.

The three of us head for lunch when the service concludes. We settle in at a nice pizza joint called Pizzicato.

"I'm glad to see you again," Jack tells me, peering over the menu in his hands.

Jack really does remind me of my own grandfather. I think that's why I like him as much as I do. He's older than I realize and his fragility frightens me. I fear for Maraye. We're children in comparison to Jack.

"You should bring a telescope over to the farm, Emmett," he tells me. "Our loft balcony would be perfect for star-gazing. Sometimes I go out to sit on it and catch Maraye just lying there singing to herself. She could use some company."

"Grandpa!" Maraye squeals. Her face has turned scarlet red. "Are you trying to kill me?"

"That sounds great," I laugh. "We'll have to do that sometime. I've been anxious to hear her sing."

"Oh Emmett, she sings like an angel," he jokes, patting Maraye on the back.

Maraye is still recovering from Jack's earlier statement, "Grandpa, I'm not going anywhere with you anymore," she says, covering her face in embarrassment.

"Oh, relax," he tells her. "Emmett doesn't care. Besides, the two of you could use some more social interaction. You're a bunch of recluses. When I was your age, I had six girlfriends."

Maraye explodes into laughter. "You did not! You married grandma when you were seventeen."

"Well, I would have, if I had been single," he responds.

It takes little observation to deduce that their love for each other is strong. Their love for each other drowns out the loud stir of the restaurant. I feel a sting of pain as I think to myself that I won't know that kind of love again. The ache swells as they share stories of Maraye's childhood and the past with me. I hear a hint of remorse in their voices as they tell stories of Jack's wife and Maraye's mother. They've lost much but they sustain each other regardless.

"What were you like as a child?" Jack asks me.

"Me? I was quiet. I mostly kept to myself. I read sci-fi novels and played chess with my grandpa."

"Do you have any family?"

"They're gone," I say politely, not wanting to sound like it bothers me.

"So you've been looking after yourself for a while, haven't you?"

"Yeah, but it's not so bad. I'm used to it and I have my studies. Well, I had my studies. I read a lot now. I had friends," I tell him wanting to ease the tension.

"I mean I have friends. I left them behind though. We'd break into this Old Catholic school back home and drink beers together. We'd whine about girls and sing songs, skateboard and that sort of thing."

Jack smiles at me. He's onto my act, but he plays along.

"That's nice," he says, "it's good to have friends."

"Yeah ..." I mutter, staring at the pizza in front of me. "It is ..."

"Sometimes I worry about you, all alone out at the cabin," he says. "Loneliness can strangle you, if you aren't careful."

"Oh, I'm okay. I'm sure some of my pals will visit soon," I lie. I smile at them, playing my part.

I'd like to think that more power exists in the love between Maraye and Jack than the anguish sending me on my way. I just can't convince myself. Nevertheless, their bond moves me. It's rare to see genuine unconditional love like the kind they share. But its power seems almost infallible. I'm drawn to it.

"I want to hear more about young Emmett," Maraye says, putting me back on the spot.

I laugh and sip on my soda. I take a bite of pepperoni and think for a moment.

"Well, like I said I was just a normal kid, only more-so I guess. I had some friends. We were close growing up. We'd just chase girls and look out for each other. Mostly I just read books and studied. I was a dreamer."

"What were you like, Maraye?" I ask wanting to shift the focus to her. She laughs, scratching her head and nervously twiddling her fingers.

"I guess I was quiet," she says, taking a swig of her Dr. Pepper. "I don't know. I kept to myself for the most part. I liked to be outdoors. I was a dreamer too, I guess. I liked to roam the forest, dreaming of adventures. I dreamed about seeing the world." She stares off out the window behind me. Jack chuckles but the look he gives me is odd. I think he might feel guilty about Maraye staying in Paris.

"She had boys after her constantly," he laughs.

"I don't doubt that for a second," I say laughing and fighting back a slight feeling of jealousy. Maraye's smiling at me with a glint in her eye. I think she's trying to judge my reaction.

Jack breaks the tension and keeps the conversation rolling. "Were you close to your grandfather, Emmett?"

"Yeah ..." I say, letting the past roll over me. "We were very close. I got my love of learning from him. He taught me to read well and examine things."

I pause and relish the feeling of love I have for my grandfather. It's nice to feel something positive about the past for a change.

"He told me of his youth," I continue. "He spent it here on a cabin by the lake. It's where he met my grandmother. My own mother spent her summers here as well. By coming here I feel like I'm just following in their footsteps. They found something spiritual in the woods and the lakes. But that was another life," I lament.

Maraye and Jack are looking at me, their eyes full of pity. Maraye looks as though she's about to cry. I fight off the desire to lunge for the door and head for the interstate. I can see in their faces that they actually hurt for me. I'm pissed at myself for getting personal.

"Yes," Jack says. "Sometimes, we need to go somewhere quiet. Where better than here?" he laughs. "Well, in any regard, we're glad you came."

Jack truly is a good human being. The rest of our meal is a lament of lost adolescence and ruined dreams. Strangely, they don't turn their sorrow into cynicism. They just suck the sweetness from it and let it be. They don't seem angry like I am.

I wish I could find a way out like they have, a way to handle the tragedies of existence. Driving back with Maraye next to me is a pleasant, albeit, terrifying distraction. She grins at me when the rough terrain forces her skin to brush mine. I grin back and wink. Our attraction to each other shines through my unhappiness like insect wings in the sun.

She stays behind when Jack leaves and we walk on a path in the forest. It follows the edge of the lake for a few miles, and then circles around to the edge of my driveway. I could walk with her until my feet crack. The conversation flows and flows. We never miss a step. She shares her memories of the forest with me.

"I remember walking through this spot with my mom when I was younger. Grandpa would fish for most of the day and we'd clean them and have a cookout.

"That sounds like heaven. You must miss those days." I say.

"Yes, I do."

She smiles, running her fingers through the leaves of an oak, beside her. "Some days, more than others, but I was lucky to have them," she finishes optimistically.

The smell of pine and bark drifts through the air. The weak breeze feels nice.

"My grandpa finds you very interesting," says.

"Me? What could he possibly find interesting about me?" I ask incredulously.

She casually kicks some leaves and dirt as we stroll, shrugging her shoulders.

"Who knows?" she jokes. But he thinks this place can help you. He kept going on about being here to help you. He thinks your paths were meant to cross. He thinks God sent you here to us. I don't know …" she says, avoiding eye contact.

"God? I don't think God and I are on speaking terms. Besides, if there is a God, he's probably just as confused about all this mess as we are. So I say damn him. Damn him for letting this mess happen down here. Of course if the Christians are right, he's probably damning me too," I tell her sarcastically.

She laughs and bumps me with her shoulder. The dry leaves crunch and crack beneath our feet.

"Emmett, why are you always so angry? I think most people mean well. I'm sure they're just afraid to admit they're afraid. Not everyone has the courage to look around at all this like you do. It's easier for people to pretend they know than for them to admit they don't know. That's a scary place to be."

Her compassion makes me smile. She has a way of appealing to the empathetic part of me.

"I'm sorry, Maraye. You're right. I am an asshole, aren't I?"

"Only sometimes," she laughs. I smile when I notice her biting down on her lip.

After a while my head starts to feel light. I had a bit too much whiskey before we started walking. It's taking a toll. Regardless, Maraye helps distract me from the ache.

"What's it like to be so free?" she asks me.

"Free? What do you mean?"

She breathes deep and sighs. We stop in a clearing on the side of the lake. The cattails are all flattened from a recent storm so we have a clear view of the water.

"You don't worry about money and you can go anywhere you want. What's that like?"

"Oh that ... I guess it would be nice if circumstances were different. It's hard to be free like that without suffering unless you're fabulously wealthy like a movie star or something. Freedom like that comes at a price. I mean it's a consequence for people who don't have a reason to be somewhere, living life with someone they love."

"Yes, I guess that makes sense," Maraye says as we round a corner into the driveway.

Just as she's about to begin speaking again, I notice a brown silhouette. There's a dog sitting on the porch as if he's lived here all his life. His fur is light brown and he's caked in mud. I think he's a spaniel of some sort. He sees us approaching and remains sitting. He's just staring at us. His tongue wags, to and fro.

"Where did you come from, little guy? Maraye asks, rubbing his belly. He looks at me, takes a step toward me with his head down, and pushes against my feet.

"Can we keep him?" Maraye asks, excited and giggly like an adolescent schoolgirl.

"Sure ..." I say, grinning and running my hands over his matted coat. "I've thought about getting a dog before actually. Oh god, he needs a bath. He smells like dirty laundry."

We coax him into the house and I lift him into the tub. At the end of his bath all three of us are covered in soap and water. He sits with us on the couch in front of the television as we watch old music videos. I try to sing the words right through the blur of whiskey.

I wouldn't normally sing in front of Maraye but we shared a glass of American Honey as we were bathing the dog and now we're halfway through another. Our new arrival seemed like a good excuse for a celebration.

"Without all of these things I can do, but without your love I won't make it through!" My words are slurred and out of tune.

She laughs at my singing and takes my hand. I twirl her and the dog barks running between us. From the outside looking in we might appear to be a happy little family. The thought appeals to me but I quickly think of Lenai.

"What are we going to name the dog?" she asks, trying to take a sip of whiskey without spilling her glass. I think of a name between twirls.

"How about Charlie?" I ask. "He seems like a Charlie to me."

She stumbles and laughs. "Why Charlie?"

"It was my grandpa's middle name," I tell her.

"I like it. Hi, Charlie!" she says, bending down and picking him up. "Emmett, I'm so dizzy! Dance with us!"

She's beautiful and true as we dance and sing and drink through the night. I'm in control of my emotions tonight. It's a welcome change. My attention is fixed solely on Maraye and Charlie as we dance our troubles away. We trade swigs from a bottle until it's empty.

"Maraye, you should really start dancing again," I tell her as she pirouettes in front of me.

"You think so? Would you come see me?" she asks.

"Hell, yeah …" I say. Especially if you keep moving your hips like that."

"Emmett! You pervert!" She's laughing and it makes me grin.

"Would you help me rehearse?"

"Of course."

"Would you cheer me on?"

"Always."

We tire out after a while and sit on the porch watching the rain come in droves, pounding the lake.

"If this isn't nice, I don't know what is …" Maraye whispers.

I smile at her. Charlie sits next to my feet breathing softly. I feel the dark, dank cold drifting over me as I walk into the house to pour myself a drink. Looking up at the window over the sink, I see my reflection. I see the image of a man divided.

Maraye is standing in the doorway. Her eyes look like they can topple mountains. She walks toward me, biting her lip. My stomach drops and I feel blood coursing through my body.

"Can I sleep here tonight?" Her question takes me by surprise but I'm relieved. In my subconscious I was desperate for her to stay. I'm always desperate for her to stay now.

"Of course," I say. "I'll make a bed on the couch. You can have my bed." She stares me down with her green eyes.

"Will you stay with me until I fall asleep? Storms scare me."

"Okay, yeah."

I can't take my eyes off of her as she rests. Her high cheekbones cause her cheeks to bubble as she rests her face on her folded hands. When I sleep I dream of the two of us in some far off place. I don't recognize the landscape. It's open and green. The skies are dark and blue. It's early morning. I'm lying on the ground in the dirt. It sounds as though I'm near running water. There's blood soaking the ground around me. I don't move or speak. Maraye just sits next to me, staring at my corpse.

"You were so hell-bent on understanding the unknowable," she says, stroking the hair from my lifeless face. "Answers were never what you needed, Emmett."

She begins to cry and it makes me ache, even in my sleep.

I awake in the dark. I hear the rain sliding down the kitchen window. The thunder in the distance is loud. It sounds like a war raging in the heavens. I stand and walk from the living room to the bedroom. Maraye is sleeping quietly. Charlie is curled up next to her. This is the portrait of a happy man's life. It's my life but it's not the life I planned. I can't find peace in it. It's just another ironic taunt from some invisible torturer.

When a moment like this brings something other than pure ecstasy, something must be wrong. Some powerful force is holding me at bay, keeping me from giving myself to this life, keeping me from being content. It seems to me that there are many things in life that will never lose their power. One of those things is death. I move silently across the room and sit in the old rocking chair, staring at the window, letting the calm permeate into my thoughts. The rain quietly taps to the tempo of nature's melody as the trees groan from the force of the wind.

It's much like a night I spent with Lenai back in Brooklyn. It's hard to trust the way I recall things with all the cracks in my memory growing thicker and thicker. We sat in the comfort of my flat, our shelter from the storm outside. She was tired and clinging to me for comfort. These were pure moments and there is no force with enough power to rob me of the happiness I felt that night. I believe I could have that with Maraye right now if I would let myself. A part of me thinks that I may be experiencing it anyway to some degree.

The goodness she brings to life is different than Lenai. It's not better or worse, just different. She reminds me of the days before all of this, the days when my happiness kept thoughts of death and futility at bay. There is no retrieving that innocence, that naiveté. It was swept away like leaves in a gutter. My stomach suffers when I contemplate that I will undoubtedly, living or otherwise, steal that from Maraye. I can't be whole for her and the pain of Lenai's death hasn't receded so much that I've decided against suicide.

I search at the root of the problem for something to blame, anything other than myself. I find nothing and I turn to forgetfulness, staring blankly out the window, thinking of a different life. Eventually I stop dreaming of a different life, and think of my own life. The full arc of my life moves before my eyes. I'm born. I love some people. They die. I die. The end.

The clouds are moving swiftly. I catch a glimpse of the full moon for a brief second. It's gone again, replaced by gray. The room has grown cold so I walk into the living room and return wrapped in a blanket. Maraye is awake, holding herself up, looking at me. Her eyes are groggy and she's squinting. I smile.

"You alright?" She asks while pulling the blanket to her chin.

"Yes, I just don't sleep well some nights."

"Most nights," she corrects me knowingly.

"Most nights," I concede. "Go back to sleep, I'm okay."

"Okay." She whispers, turning on her side toward me. "Just be near me. It makes me feel better."

I'm in the same room with her. She doesn't know how far off I am. I'm traveling back to far before Lenai's death. I'm up all night and I find no answers in the past or in hypothetical futures. I scour my memory searching for people I've known who have suffered. I can't see any pattern in their coping mechanisms.

It seems to me that all grief is unique in a way. At least each person's experience and adjustment or lack thereof is unique. There are some things that unite the suffering. Our fear that we'll lose our memories, for instance: I'm certain that we all share this fear. Pictures lose their power. Eventually we all roam around hoping that some happenstance will spark genuine recollection.

It's the small things. The unexpected simple things in life that bring me back. The way a person smiles or walks through the streets. The smell of the air or a certain perfume, or the position of the sun and moon in the sky. All of these things serve as constants, carrying me back to moments in the past, however briefly.

My greatest fear stems from stupid myths like heaven and hell. The horror tears right through me despite my doubt and disbelief. If only Christians would reform the pictures they paint with images more loving and hopeful. I would die just to hear that Lenai is somewhere safe. I would die to know that she's all right, that she's happier wherever she's gone. I've accepted that there is no provable assurance about anything related to faith. But I am beginning to believe that consciousness carries on.

I press my hand against the window, hoping that Lenai is being looked after if she still exists in some form. With all that I've been through I still resolve to continue searching for answers, for reasons, for meaning, for anything that can sustain me. How I wish Maraye could set me free from the torture.

I'm weary of this endless riddle. I rest here and admire Maraye as she sleeps. I'm crazy about her moon-pale skin. There must be a way to cope with my fear so that I can be with her and be at peace with life.

CHAPTER 7

December has arrived. The air is a constant chill now and the sky has turned a steady gray. Maraye visits often but things remain platonic. She doesn't seem to mind. She'll sit quietly on the couch and knit while I work my way through Lewis's, *A Grief Observed*.

The dimly lit cabin and heated white pine conjure solitude for the two of us. Maraye sleeps over quite a bit. She sleeps in my empty bed. She's had several fits over my insistence to sleep on the floor. I haven't had the heart to answer her demands for an explanation. I simply insist that I prefer the floor and that she should just let it be.

Truthfully, I've grown quite dependent on her. She forces me to visit her at work, so she knows I'm eating enough. I'm not sure how exactly she managed to rope me in the way she has. It's possible that I haven't been sober enough to identify it but I feel something different when I glance over from my book to see her wrapped in a quilt, smiling at me.

We eat together. We sleep near each other. But I'm not entirely here. I don't think I'll ever be here entirely. In my heart I don't think I'll ever be set free from the pain, or at least that's what I keep telling myself. Sometimes I go half a day without thinking of Lenai. The pain still rests in me like a dull throb that I've become accustomed to living with after enduring it for so long.

Regrettably, the thoughts of Lenai, when they do come, have become so painful that I'm constantly drunk, more than ever before. I do my best to hide it from Maraye, but she almost always knows. It's gotten to the point that the guilt of my drunkenness has me hiding bottles of whiskey throughout the cabin. I'll need it more than ever as Christmas approaches.

My intentions are to ignore this season until it passes but Maraye and Jack have other plans. I simply don't have the will power to put up a fight. They need this as much as I don't need it. This will be the second Christmas since Lenai was killed. She died on December sixteenth, a week from today on a drizzly Wednesday morning. I feel the cold of that day every time I step outside.

Tonight Maraye is making split pea soup for the two of us. Jack and I taught her to play poker last month, and she insists on playing it with me every chance she has. She's progressing just fine. By all accounts she's as intelligent as she is gorgeous. She had cable of some sort installed in the living room. I despise television but we do enjoy watching science programs and discussing them together. In an effort to increase my interest in fishing she often turns on fishing programs at opportune moments.

Truthfully I just enjoy being on the water with her. Some mornings when we don't sleep we'll go out before sunrise. The way her skin glows translucent in the early light holds my thoughts at bay until we succumb to exhaustion and sleep the day away. She has no idea the beauty that she gives this place.

Maraye is looking at me tonight as we sit at the table. She's suppressing a laugh.

"Emmett, your clothes are wrecked. I think we should get you some new ones. Immediately …" She laughs. "You should let me help you."

She's not out of line. I'm helpless with these petty things. The flannel shirt I'm wearing is starting to tear at the elbows and there are holes forming.

Smiling at her, I jest in response. "Do I look like a lumberjack?"

She lights up laughing hard. "Only a little! But I think you're handsome, regardless."

It's a genuine slip of the tongue. A look of horror and embarrassment shoots across my face. Looking up I see her staring at me, frozen and uncertain. In a stroke of chivalry I decide to join her in embarrassment.

"It's alright, Maraye, I think you're gorgeous."

Her face is as red as my shirt. Judging by the amount of blood I feel rush to my face, I can only assume that mine matches hers. Her lips are a soft pink and they're shaking fiercely. I'm dizzy from the alcohol and this doesn't help matters. A large part of me wants to kill myself from the guilt and anguish warring within me. Another part of me wants to jump across the table to kiss her.

I can't do this. I feel Lenai's memory rise to the surface of my thoughts.

She must see the way my face falls because she speaks quickly. "There you go running off again. What are you afraid of, Emmett?"

I'm silent as Charlie approaches under the table. I run my fingers through his fur and look down at him to avoid making eye contact with Maraye.

I stand up and walk to the far wall behind the table. Glancing at Maraye I collapse against it with my head between my legs. The song *Lonely People* is playing softly on the kitchen radio.

This is for all the lonely people, thinking that life has passed them by.

"Don't let the memory kill you," she says to me from the table.

"Maraye …" I breathe, barely audible.

"Emmett, don't do that. Just stay with me tonight. Be here with me tonight."

The sound of her whisper and the scent of her perfume lull me into relaxation. Effortlessly she moves across the room and sits next to me. She rests her head on my shoulder. We've haven't touched in weeks; denying my desire is excruciating. I feel the ache in my ribs. I'd let her rest in me until I die if I could. But things are never that simple and my despair beckons. We just sit in silence for what seems like eternity. She listens to my breathing.

Maraye's head jerks up as a knock sounds from the front door. I squeeze her hand and stand to answer the door, thinking that Jack has come to visit. I pull open the door and find myself face to face with Sonya Cooper, Lenai's mother.

"Hello, Emmett," she smiles.

"Hello, Sonya," I reply, wanting to turn and run.

Her eyes fill with moisture and she gives me a once over, no doubt taking notice of my despondent state.

She steps forward and hugs me. She looks healthy. Her hair is straight and well kept. She's wrapped in a rose colored cardigan.

Oddly it feels as though the young fire gone out within me is reignited. In a certain sense, a piece of Lenai lives on and is here with me now. I have no words for Sonya and the grief she stirs inside me can't be described. She pulls the past into the present. But I am glad to see her.

"I'm sorry to drop in like this. I didn't know how to reach you other than snail mail. I just figured I'd try the address on the last letter you wrote. I'm on my way to Kansas City, to see my sister for Christmas. I wanted to stop by and see how you're doing," she explains as I close the door behind her.

"Don't be sorry. I'm glad you came. I've missed you," I tell her, truthfully.

"Oh, hello," Sonya says, looking past me to Maraye.

"Hi there ..." Maraye waves nervously. She looks like a deer in headlights.

"This is my friend, Maraye," I say, trying to sound casual.

"I'll give you two some privacy," Maraye says as she climbs to her feet.

I throw her an apologetic look and she smiles slightly before disappearing into the bedroom.

"Do you want some tea?" I ask. "I have several different kinds. Maraye really likes tea."

"Sure, do have chamomile?"

"Actually, that's my favorite."

I fumble through the cabinets, pulling out the tea bags. Sonya's presence makes my grief feel fresh. It feels like yesterday I was meeting her with Lenai for the first time. I remember being nervous and twitchy on the way to meet her. Lenai wore a plaid skirt with a white top and black sunglass.

I remember everything.

Sonya sits patiently as I cross the room. She sets her purse on the ottoman and looks around the room.

"Thank you," she says as I pour hot water from the coffee maker into a couple of mugs. A few moments later I hand her a mug and sit next to her. I'm unsure of how to speak to her. I look up from my tea to see her looking at me with a sort of pained expression painted across her face.

"She's cute, Emmett. Are you guys together?" she asks, motioning toward my bedroom.

"No, it's not like that. We're friends. We look after each other," I explain.

She sips her tea and purses her lips gently.

"That's good. I'm glad you aren't completely alone. How're you hanging in there?"

Her pitiful expression makes me want to pull myself apart. I'm offended that she seems to be okay with the thought of me moving on from Lenai with Maraye.

"I'm alright," I respond.

Lying to people I love is becoming second nature.

"How are you, really?" She frowns at me, telling me that she's unconvinced.

I trace my hairline with my fingertips. It's going to be one of those nights.

"You look different," she says glancing at me. "You look tired, Emmett. What are you doing out here hiding from the world?"

"I'm not hiding. I'm looking for something. I'm trying to figure things out, I guess. I like it out here. It's nice and quiet."

"Your fire's gone out Emmett. I can see it just looking at you. Why don't you write me anymore?" She genuinely sounds saddened that I stopped writing. The truth is that I was mostly too drunk and I couldn't bring myself to write her.

"I just miss her," I mutter pathetically.

"I miss her, too. We all miss her, Emmett, but it's been two years now. You need to live your life. I know it won't heal completely ..."

"No," I cut her off, anger breaking my composure.

I can't believe she's telling me to move on and heal as if Lenai were some passing phase in our lives. She was my life. She was my future.

"You seem to be getting along just fine without her. I'm glad for that but pardon me for having a rough go of it," I say evenly, putting my tea down and standing to my feet.

I feel like the oceans have all dried up. I want to be left alone. I don't need anyone telling me how to feel. The way Sonya looks at me makes me feel like I've committed a heinous crime.

"Is this how you treat people now? If you continue to live without love you'll end up drinking yourself to death, Emmett. Is that what you want? Because it looks to me like there are people who need you. That girl back in that room must be fond of you. What about her? Lenai would want you to treat her right."

"I told you that it's not like that."

Sonya stares at me sternly and stands to her feet. The weight of her questioning strikes a nerve. Somewhere inside me a sun is dying and exploding. Whatever gentleness I had because of Lenai is gone. I'm pissed off.

"Listen, I don't know what the fuck Lenai wants! She sure as hell wouldn't want me to be with another girl! She's dead and you and everyone else seem to have forgotten that! She was alive once! Remember that? Remember when she was living and breathing? Do you remember when you had a daughter at all? Because I remember everything, every single fucking thing! You don't think I ask myself those questions every goddamn day of my aimless life? I have to stay drunk just to stop thinking about her!"

Sonya quickly crosses the distance between us and her hand whips across my face like a scorpion tail. I know I deserve it. I deserve much worse for what I've said to this woman. The constant guilt has made a wreck of my soul. This only adds to it. Her face is red and her eyes are glaring into me.

"You sit down and listen to me," she says, her finger in my face, her arms shaking. "I know you think you can't live without her love. But you haven't lost it, and deep down you know that. So what are you afraid of, Emmett? Are you afraid that life will take your memories from you? It won't. Do you think letting yourself feel happiness will invalidate your love for her? It won't. You're a damn fool if you can't see that. You've convinced yourself that you love her by living in your grief. You can't live like this. You can't live without love. It's worse than death."

Her words are a scalpel cutting away. I stumble to the counter, tears covering my face. Without even looking I grasp the bottle of American Honey and feel the whiskey drip down my throat. I don't even notice the burn anymore. I feel myself cough some up so I drink deeper.

"Oh, Emmett ..." I hear Sonya lament behind me. I turn and feel her arms wrap around me. I return the embrace, nearly collapsing as I bury my head in her shoulder.

"I'm so sorry," I whisper, barely audible. "It was my fault, Sonya. She'd be here ... did my promises mean anything, Sonya?"

I feel her warm tears on my collarbone.

"It's not your fault. It's no one's fault. You can't live with that. No force on earth can keep her love from you or yours from her — not even death. You kept your promises to her while she was here. You don't need to keep them anymore. There's no one here to keep them for. She's gone. " She blinks as she grasps my face in her hands. Tiny anointed tears flow across her cheekbones and down her chin.

"I don't think I can love anymore," I say to her. "Something inside me broke. It's gone. Sonya, I don't want to live anymore. I can't get it back. Our love was supposed to be infallible but it's gone. I'm ruined. I don't want to be here without her." The truth pours out of me and Sonya stares back, looking heartbroken.

She wraps her hands tighter around my face. "You're a good man, Emmett. You can choose to love and you have to choose life. You need to live fully. It's the only way you can keep love alive. You have to choose it. Certainly it will leave you bruised but you can't be you without it and people need you to be yourself. You can honor Lenai by living a good life and loving the best that you can. That's all any of us can do."

"I'm sorry," I tell her while I put away the whiskey bottle. "I'm just lost without her here."

"Hang in there, Emmett. Things will get better," she assures me. "Tell me what I can do. How can I help you?"

"You can't do anything. I've got to do this on my own."

I spend a couple more hours with Sonya, showing her around the lake and telling her about Paris. She doesn't stay long because she wants to make it to St. Louis tonight. She makes me promise to write and I leave her my number so she can reach me. When she leaves I walk back to my bedroom and find Maraye asleep under the covers.

It pains me to know she heard my hysterics. I pull the covers over her shoulders. The anguish cuts through me when my hand feels her moist pillow. I don't want to be away from her so I take up my chair across the room. This is my fault. I allowed this hurt to come on her. A nice thought crosses my mind, that one day I could be strong enough to care for Maraye, but the next thought reminds me: I don't think I'll ever let this go.

Tonight I wish to God I could find some rest. The familiar white pine floods my nostrils. Maraye's soft breathing puts me at ease. I'm tempted to cross the room and give her all that's left of me. I'm able to put my thoughts together in a more concise way. It's not long before I make up my mind about what to do next. I can't stay here and hurt her again.

The past taunts me as I drift off. It's nice to fall asleep near Maraye. This may be the last night that I can enjoy this comfort.

In the morning I wake her with breakfast. Even with her hair a mess she's gorgeous in the morning light. She lets out a half smile as we eat, waiting for me to speak. I can tell that she's distant.

"I'm sorry about last night. I didn't mean for that to happen. I didn't mean for you to hear that."

"You lied to me," she says looking up at me.

"What do you mean?" I ask.

"You told me that you didn't have any family," she says quietly, sipping her orange juice.

"Sonya isn't family," I tell her.

"She certainly seemed like family to me. She cares about you like family. Most people wish their family loved them as much as she seems to love you."

"Well she isn't family, Maraye. I'll lose track of her like everyone else."

"That's a nice way to view things, Emmett. You can't even see what's right in front of you. You'll only ever think of Lenai. You'll never see me, will you?"

I knew this was coming. I've been dreading the day Maraye would finally make me choose her over Lenai's memory. That makes what I have to say next even harder to get out.

"Maraye ... I ... I ... Maraye, I'm going to Nassau for a while." She looks up at me with puffy red eyes.

"You're leaving?" she asks, in borderline shock.

"Yes. I'm sorry."

"Are you coming back?" she asks. Her voice is suddenly colder than I've heard before.

"Yes."

"Good ..." she says, evenly. "I hope you work things out. You need to get some perspective before you lose the good things you have left. You need to make up your mind about us, about what we are."

"What we are? I thought we were friends."

"Friends, Emmett? Friends don't play house and sleep over with each other. I can't wait forever, just hoping you have feelings for me. I'd wait for you, Emmett. I get that you need time, but you have to give me something. You need to ask me to wait for you, or talk to me, or ... anything ..." she says, her voice catching. "You know what it's like for me? I never know if you're just going to bail on me for good. Do you know how I feel, how fucking sick I feel waiting to see if you care about me the way I care about you? Or do you ever even think of me? Do you ever stop thinking of her?" She's crying steadily and wiping her face with a towel now.

"Maraye, I do think about you. Fuck ... I need to get out of here and clear my head. This is what I was afraid of. I'm screwing everything up."

She smothers her face with the towel and removes it. "You're not very good to the people who care about you. You know that? You're a defeatist asshole. Never mind ..." She walks away, disappearing into the bathroom.

"I know ..." I say to myself as I bury my face in my hands.

I doze off on the couch while Maraye is showering. When I wake up she's gone. She's left a note on the counter for me. I read it slowly as I sip on some tea.

I'll be waiting for you to come back to me, Emmett. I can wait a bit longer for you. I just want you to know that you're the best person I've ever known. I'm very fond of you and I'm sorry for losing my temper. Have fun and I hope you find some peace. I have Charlie. – Maraye.

I want to tell her that I'll miss her but I stop myself from calling her. The less affection I show, the less attached she'll become. I fold up the note and put it in my pocket before I head to the bedroom to pack. Tomorrow I'll head to the airport and make for Nassau.

CHAPTER 8

Josef is surprised when I appear in the doorway of his home. The look on his face is one of genuine happiness. It's an extraordinary thing to be reunited with someone who's sincerely happy to see me. He's wearing his usual Jitney guide uniform.

"You're alive, old friend!" His arms squeeze me tightly. I return the gesture, afraid of the news that I've brought with me. My eyes swell as I pull away from our embrace.

"Where's Lenai?" he asks me, still smiling and looking behind me toward the street. "Did she come with you?"

I don't know how to tell him. He's so happy to see me.

"Josef ..." I try to speak, to tell him that my love is gone for all time. The room is shrinking. "She's gone Josef. She's dead."

I feel the firm grasp of Josef's weathered hand on my shoulder. He sits down slowly in the chair beside me. Tears roll down his cheeks. Strange as it sounds, it's comforting to have someone suffer alongside me. It's strange to see the weight of the news crushing someone so long after her death. For some time I've felt as though I'm the last of my kind, the only person still suffering.

Josef looks at me with frosty eyes full of sorrow. "I am sorry my friend. I am sorry for your heart. One day at a time. One day at a time ..." His sadness burns through me like a fever.

It's later than I expected. We just sit here together in silence for an hour or so. The silvery moonlight shines on us through the small windows in the kitchen. Nassau is on fire tonight. The island seems to be ablaze with lovers and cheer. Island songs ring out through the air.

The voices shout out:

"This land is your land; this land is my land,

From Grand Bahama *down to* Inagua

From the Berry Islands, *down to* Mayaguana

This land is made for you and me"

Lenai would sing along if she were here. I find a little comfort in knowing that I still remember what she was like. At one point during our mournful silence I swear I hear her voice singing out. I don't linger in the reverie as long as Josef does. His grief is still fresh.

Josef's mourning period is cut short when his youngest son returns from work. Kylie is only sixteen but he works at the market for one of the larger merchants. He sells cheap knockoffs of name brand watches and purses. The shirt he is changing into makes me grin. It's covered in a large picture of the rapper known as Ice Cube. He greets me with a handshake but rushes off to see a girl.

"Kylie has a girlfriend," Josef tells me with a smirk.

"Idiot kids ..." I laugh.

"Let's eat," he says, standing and walking a few feet into the kitchen.

I don't need to ask what we're having and I'm not surprised when Josef tells me. Conch is a kind of sea snail. The locals claim it's an aphrodisiac. Josef has eight children and he swears up and down that it's from eating conch all his life. The first time I had conch was in a soup. Lenai and I were swimming a few hundred feet from shore when a man offered to cook it for us from his boat. We did not know it was a snail.

As we eat I explain my exile to Paris. I tell Josef all about the trees and the lake. He tells me he'd like to see snow in person someday. He wants to see frost on the ground and the effect of warm breath on cold air. We laugh together as I joke about pissing in the snow. I tell him a little about Maraye.

Heat drifts over my skin. I feel the calm that I had come here seeking. Lenai feels close, just like I had hoped.

"Emmett, what are you doing here? I know you didn't come here just to see my handsome face. What are you looking for?" he asks. He slurps his soup loudly.

"I wanted to see you, actually. I wanted to feel Lenai." I can't look him in the eyes.

"So you came here to remember the life you loved?" Josef shifts in his chair and looks at me. "Nassau is a long way to come just to torture yourself. Do you feel her?"

I speak my mind, somewhat surprised by what I say. "Yes, at least in certain moments. I feel guilty whenever the pain alleviates. I had to come here; she's starting to feel distant the more I become attached to Maraye. Sometimes I forget what she smelled like. I forget the sound of her voice or I can't quite picture her right in my mind. I can't remember the clothes she wore. It feels like I'm betraying her. It's eating me alive. I can't make sense of it."

"Do you love her?" he asks.

"With all that I am ..." I reply. Even as I respond I feel relieved.

Josef smiles at me as he rests his hand on my shoulder.

"Time can cause many things to wax and wane, including your memory. But it cannot wear down your love for each other. That's yours," he tells me. "You own that love. It was a choice you made. Nothing can undo that but you. My wife has been gone for ten long years and I love her now, just as much as I did on our wedding day. You were robbed of many happy years with her and for that I am deeply sorry. But I know that she would want you to have a life of happy years. She would not want this suffering for you. She wouldn't want you to be afraid."

Josef's Bahamian accent is thick. But his words are clear. He gets up from the table and collects the dishes.

"Let's go for a walk, friend," he says.

We head toward Cable Beach, and as we walk I take in the beauty that is all around me. I remember the first time I saw all this."What do I do without her, Josef?" I sound like a child pleading for help. Josef places his hand on my shoulder, giving me a firm shake.

"What do you think Lenai would want you to do? Would she want you to just give up? Emmett, I'm not a fool. I know you're considering it. How do you think giving up would affect the ones who need you? Are you willing to send them to the same sad place you're in now?"

I don't respond. Ahead of us a couple strolls under the streetlights, holding hands and resting in each other. Across the street a family pours out of a theater laughing and smiling together. It's nice to find a crowd. Crowds are hard to come by in Paris. I can't help but wonder if Maraye is thinking of me back in Paris.

We're making our way through Olde Towne where all the tourists shop and eat near the beach. Josef waits for me as I stop off to get Maraye some souvenirs. Hopefully jewelry or something of the sort puts her in the forgiving mood when I return.

We leave a gift shop with a bag of Conch shells. Before we continue our walking, I stop off and get a few shots and a drink to go. I continue walking with Josef, my hand filled with a green Vesper. A green Vesper is a variation of a Vesper martini. It's an amalgamation of gin, vodka and absinthe. I started drinking it after reading about it in a James Bond book. It warms my bones.

The sky is filled with light and the air full of songs. The wind carries the aroma of Latakia and Fire-Cured tobacco. The streets grow less populated. The songs grow faint and the stars brighten as we move away from the crowd. I began to imagine a silhouette of my lost love moving through the haze toward me. Josef's grizzled tenor breaks the spell.

"Do you still love the night sky?"

"Yes," I say, glancing up. The stars shine like silver coins.

"Do you still explore it the way you did before?"

"Not so much ..." I say.

"Why not? What happened to your passion?" Josef purses his lips at me and looks back up to the night sky.

"I don't know. Life came and turned my gaze elsewhere."

My answer brings a sorrow to me. I have missed the fascination I once carried.

"That's a shame," Josef says. "You need to be passionate about things. You cared about science before you knew Lenai, right?"

"Yeah ..." I tell him, the sorrow still bothering me. "I just can't seem to take my mind off death these days. I don't know what to do about it. Everything's just so pointless."

"You know that's a lie, don't you? And you're going to be very familiar with death if you continue with that lethal drinking. How long have you been a drinking like that?" His tone is serious and the look on his face tells me he knows I'm not drinking casually.

"Lenai dies and I'm not allowed to drink?" I ask bitterly.

He stops walking and looks me in the eye. "You shouldn't be drinking this much. How do you expect to find what you're searching for if you're drinking like a sailor? How do you even know you have clear thoughts? Drinking to be a drunk isn't the way to handle sadness, Emmett."

"Point taken," I say reluctantly.

This is the first time I've even stopped to consider if my drinking is damaging. If I insist on duking it out with the mysteries of the universe, I should at least have a clear head. I'm not resigned to being a drunk. I just haven't had the courage to face my pain sober.

"Listen my friend: no one can help you if you don't choose to help yourself." He casually rests his hand on my shoulder, looking into my eyes. "You're better than a drunk but this is your journey," he says. "Lenai would want better for you. Pull yourself together."

"I know, Josef. I know."

"Now," he says, grinning at me. "Tell me more about this Maraye."

I can't help but smile at his demand.

"Ha!" He smiles, clapping me on my arm. "So, she's special? How does she feel about you?"

"Hey, what are we, school girls?" I ask through the embarrassment.

"Does she know that she's special to you?"

"No," I tell him. "I'm not very good to her actually."

"Are you afraid?" Judging by his tone I think he knows the answer to his question.

"Yes, I'm terrified. But I think she knows that, which is probably why she puts up with my bullshit."

"I'm sure she cuts you some slack. You're a good man. I would very much like to meet her."

"Oh, I don't know," I say, feeling guilty.

"Don't play games with her, Emmett. What are your intentions?"

"I don't know, Josef. I really don't know. I've been telling myself that I can only ever love Lenai, but Maraye and I are best friends."

"Well," he says as we walk up the steps to the main boardwalk. "You'd better figure it out. I doubt she'll wait forever."

"She won't have to," I tell him.

Josef glances at me, nodding his head. "What's special about her?"

"I like the way she dances and I like the way she sings. The way I feel when I watch her dance. I can't explain that," I confess. Behind us a family laughs and I hear some children scream. I glance back to see two young boys running through the tide.

"When she dances," I continue, "it feels like she conquers all my cynicism. I don't feel dead or empty. I don't know. I want to be with her despite everything but I can't let myself. Won't that mean that Lenai meant nothing to me?"

I stare down at my feet. Something inside me knows that's not true.

"I think you're trying to make yourself believe that because you're afraid. And Emmett, can I tell you something?"

"Of course," I say.

"You haven't stopped smiling since I asked you about Maraye."

"Shit …" I say. I hesitate a moment and then chuckle with him.

"Emmett, I think you'd be hard pressed to find anyone who ever lived who didn't suffer loss in their lifetime. The price we pay for love is steep but the price we pay for not loving, for locking ourselves away from the world, is much steeper."

"Well … fuck me …" I reply, kicking the sand and grinning.

Josef's booming laughter rattles my eardrums and I join him in laughter. We grin ear to ear and head back up the beach toward his house. For the first time in a long time I think I've stumbled onto some solid truth; finally something that makes sense to me.

A week later Josef is seeing me off on the beach.

"Be careful," he tells me as I launch off in his small fishing boat. I convinced him to let me take it out near his house. It's dark but I promise not to go far and I have plenty of light and emergency flares. The boat is only 12 feet and has an inoperable trolling motor so I have to paddle with oars. The tide is in my favor but I'm exhausted by the time I'm out far enough to relax.

It's hard to imagine coming back from this. Back there on land society is pulling people apart. Out here there is no religion, no war, and no money — just quiet. I don't want to go back to that. Of course, I'll end up back in all that shit in a few hours at best. Josef was right though; coming out here like this by myself was sheer stupidity. But I've always been that way. Tell me not to do something and I'll be finished doing it before you finish telling me not to do it.

It's all so irrelevant out here, the world's unending wars and insipid romances. Some fish, or something fairly large, has hit this stupid boat a few times. It scares me enough that I slowly peek over the edge of the boat, only to retract my head quickly out of fear. I curl up in the middle expecting some shark to launch itself to the surface.

It's a nice view looking up from my back. There are no clouds, just a big black view of nothing and everything. I've only seen the stars this well with my naked eye once before, in the desert, back in Nevada and Arizona.

I have no idea where the current is pushing me or how I'll get back to the right pier. I'm too weak and the current and waves have completely defeated me, so I'm just floating here now. I'm lost but free. That's the way I like it, though. Whatever Maraye might think I'm doing right now, she couldn't imagine this. The world's just open.

I smile because I know she's thinking of me.

It's nice to be drunk on the Atlantic Ocean. Lately I've been ending my evenings with a few shots of this cheap whiskey. It's warm and smooth. It's not hard to find good alcohol down here.

I nearly shit myself when I hear another loud thud beneath the boat. My attention is pulled away from my thoughts. I hear a choir singing off in the distance. I can't understand what they're singing but it sounds like an odd rendition of Silent Night. It's Christmas Eve. That's how I know that Maraye is thinking of me. All over the island, people are heading to mass and sharing meals with their families.

"Fuck ..." I mutter to myself, covering my face with my hands.

I'm hurting and I can no longer avoid the sorrow I feel. I should be spending Christmas with Maraye. I want to get home and make things right with her. I know what I need to do. I'm afraid but I remember what Josef told me and I believe he's right. The price we pay for not loving is steep.

This is the last night I'm going to drink. When I get home I intend to make things right with Maraye and I need to be sober to work through all of my problems. Sitting up I grasp the oars in my hands and look down into the clear water.

Merry Christmas, Maraye ... wherever you are.

Two days later Josef drives me to the airport. I'm sad to leave him but I can't stay here. I can see that he has something on his mind and my suspicion is confirmed as he slows down and stops me before we reach the terminal entrance.

"Emmett, I know that you're afraid," he says, placing his hand on my shoulder. He looks at me hard with his oak colored eyes. "But you need to understand that what makes love most meaningful is choosing to give it to someone, knowing that someday you'll suffer for it. All we really need to get through this life is someone to love and be loved by. That's it. Love is everything. Just keep that in mind. Okay?" His eyes are damp with sadness.

"Yeah, alright. I will."

"Come back when you can, Emmett," he tells me, grasping my arm tightly.

"I will. You take care of yourself," I say, fighting back tears.

"Goodbye, Emmett."

"Goodbye, Josef."

I shed a few tears as we embrace before pulling away. I wipe my face as he smiles at me and nods. I turn to head through security. It hurts to think that I might not see him again.

Twenty minutes into the flight a stewardess approaches me. "Sir, would you like a drink, something stronger than water?"

I smile and look up at her. "No thanks," I say. "I'm fine with water."

There's no one around to help me when the head ache starts. At first it comes as a dull throb but it quickly worsens into a pounding in my skull. It's agonizing but I tell myself that I can handle this. I tell myself that it isn't so bad. The last drink I had was Christmas night. I begin to rationalize having just one drink but I resist the urge. I owe it to Maraye.

I turn on an inflight movie to distract myself. Casablanca does the trick and I'm distracted most of the flight. My aim is to get back to Maraye. She'll make things better. Near the end of the flight a strange sensation begins to creep up my leg and into my arms. I can't sit still and my legs are shaking. My body begins to sweat profusely, especially around my neck. The attack passes when I exit the plane. I hurry to get back to Maraye before things get worse.

CHAPTER 9

When I get home, there's a plastic tub in front of the door. I open it to find a wrapped present with my name on a piece of paper. It's in Maraye's handwriting. I hurriedly carry my bags inside and begin to unwrap it on the kitchen counter. I recognize what it is immediately.

The top of the box reads: *The Star Theater Pro Home Planetarium.*

It's a small device that creates a visual map of the stars on the walls and ceilings of a room. Maraye and I had seen an infomercial pushing it on television one night. I lit up like a child and she clearly took notice. I move quickly to unpack her gifts and rush back outside to my truck. It's Tuesday night, which means that she's working. The café closes in half an hour so I can catch her as she leaves.

I'm only waiting about ten minutes before she emerges from the back, removing her apron and sighing. The gravel parking lot is mostly empty and the sound of her feet crossing the rocks echoes through the still night. She looks up to see me standing next to my jeep holding her presents.

"Hey ..." I say, trying not to sound desperate.

"Hey ..." she says, walking toward me. "I wasn't sure you'd want to see me anymore."

Gravel crunches loudly as one of Maraye's coworkers exits the parking lot. "I got your present ..." I tell her, smiling lightly.

I try to get my thoughts out but I rush toward her without thinking and wrap my arms firmly around her. She lets out a slight gasp but returns my embrace. She rests her head on my forehead and I feel her fingertips grasping my back.

"Maraye, I shouldn't have left. I'm sorry." She releases me and takes a step back. She inhales deeply. Her vanilla perfume washes over me.

"You did what you had to. I shouldn't have pressured you." She's being polite but it's obvious that she doesn't believe what her words suggest.

"No, don't apologize. You were right about everything." I say. "I'm a coward. You can be honest. I'm selfish and I know it. I don't want you to feel like I'm just using you or leading you on like you're some kind of pet. I care about you a lot and I should've told you that. I should have made sure you know how important you are to me. I know I'm a mess but I think that someday I may be free from all of this."

"Emmett ..." She breathes out, fighting off a smile.

"No, just let me get this out. Dammit, I've gotta get this out. I do have romantic feelings for you," I confess. "I have very strong feelings for you. I just ... I don't know if I'm going to recover from Lenai's death and I can't act on those feelings without resolving that part of me. It would be wrong of me to be with you like that until I'm sure of myself, until I'm sure that you can have me completely. I understand if you can't wait for me to get things right but that's the truth and I want you to know it. For the first time I can feel a seed of light, like maybe things can be more different than I thought."

I stop talking and Maraye steps toward me once more. Her hands wrap around my hips and she places her lips on my cheek, kissing me fiercely. She lingers and rubs her lips across my face toward my ear, sending chills through my entire body.

"I'm yours. I'll wait for you. I just want to be with you," she whispers.

Time stands still and I linger on the edge of pulling her into me and releasing all of my desire. She brushes my head with hers like a kitten and I just stand with my eyes closed, breathing in and out.

"Give me my presents," she demands, pulling back a little and smiling up at me.

I open my hands and she takes the bag and removes its contents, placing them on the hood of my jeep.

"Those are conch shells and that … that's a straw purse that some lady made herself, and that's a book about reefs," I explain nervously.

"Emmett, they're so wonderful …" she gasps, pulling a picture out of the purse and looking up at me with wide eyes.

"Yeah," I say nervously. "Josef took that picture of me. I thought you might like to have one. You don't have to keep it if you don't want to. I look like an idiot."

I'm worried that I've done something stupid because she covers her open mouth with her hands. Her eyes go misty. But she pulls me toward her, holding the picture to her chest.

"This is everything to me, Emmett. Thank you."

"You're welcome," I stutter, breathing deeply and smelling her citrus-scented hair. "I got your grandpa something too."

"Come on …" she says, pulling me toward her car. "Let's go give it to him."

"Are you sure?" I ask. I've been worried that my unexpected departure might have upset Jack.

"Of course. Come on!" She laughs, waving me toward her car.

Jack and Maraye live in an old farmhouse on thirty acres of land. It's white with red shutters and a green tin roof. Work sheds, wildflowers and a field of wheatgrass surround it. When we enter I notice a sweet smell, which distracts me from my nervousness and discomfort.

"Emmett!" Jack shouts from the living room where he's seated in a brown La-Z-Boy. "I'm glad you're back. Come in! Come in! Maraye, get him something to drink."

"I'm fine. Thanks, though," I say, walking into the living room. "I got you a present from Nassau."

"You didn't have to do that." He smirks at me as I hand him his bag. "What the hell is this?" His face twists into an amused, yet confused smile.

Maraye explodes into laughter as he pulls out a multicolored hat complimented with fake dreadlocks hanging from its back. He places the large round bowl of a hat onto his wrinkled head.

"I thought you could use a new look," I say jokingly.

"I love it, Emmett. Thank you very much." He smiles, putting it back into the bag. "So, tell me about you trip. Did you have a good time?"

Before I reply I look down to see Charlie panting next to me. "Hey boy, did you miss me?" I smile and he barks in excitement as I rub his stomach.

"I had a nice time," I tell Jack. "I ate some snails and swam a bit. It was nice, but I'm glad to be back."

"Good, I'm glad you had a nice holiday," he tells me.

"Grandpa, look what Emmett got me." Maraye butts in, changing the subject.

She proudly shows off her gifts, minus the photo. She playfully struts down an imaginary runway with her straw purse and Jack winks at me. "I see where I stand in the scheme of things," he jokes.

An hour later Maraye and I bid Jack farewell and head back to the cabin to try out my new planetarium. Charlie sits between the two of us and drools on Maraye. I let out a belly laugh at her misfortune.

"Come on, Charlie! That's disgusting! Don't laugh at me Emmett! It's not funny," she protests, pushing Charlie away.

"I need a shower," I tell Maraye as we walk inside.

"Okay, I'm just going to play with the planetarium," she says, smiling.

"Okay, I'll hurry so I can bore you with more stupid astronomy legends."

I head into the bathroom and feel it start to slither through me again. I'm feeling ill and weak. I feel like vomiting so I walk back out to the living room to talk with Maraye.

"Hey, listen. I need your help with something," I start to explain, but I'm sidetracked by the smell of something on the stove. "What are you cooking?"

"Oh!" She hops up from the table, pulling me over to the stove. "Potato soup, just for you. I thought you might be hungry when you got out of the shower."

There's enough gentleness in her eyes to bring peace in the Middle East. I've missed her. I stare at her standing in front of the stove. She smells like strawberries and cream. I can taste it on my tongue. We lock eyes.

"You're smiling, Emmett," she teases, stirring the soup and biting down on her lip.

"Sorry, I'm just starved. Anything I can do to help?" I need to get accustomed to doing household chores like cooking. I want to do nice things for Maraye.

Now I notice she's smiling as much as I am. I can't help myself and subconsciously I'm hoping she can't either. Furrowing her brow, she glances at me. "What happened to you out there, Emmett? You started to say that you needed me to help you with something. What is it?"

"Nothing," I say, not quite sure of the answer. "I think I'll hop in the shower now."

Maraye looks at me inquisitively, melting my resolve. "Alright. Are you sure you're okay? You look sweaty."

"Yeah," I say. "The last time I had anything to drink was Christmas night. I talked with Josef and I don't want to drink anymore, but I think it's starting to hit me."

"Oh, Emmett ... I'm so proud of you." She's looking at me like I'm a saint. "That's really great. I'll take care of you if you get sick. It'll be okay. Just get cleaned up and we'll relax."

"Really? That sounds great. I think a shower will help."

"Yes. You make me very happy. Did you know that?" she asks me with her hands clasped.

"I do? That's good to know."

"Yes, you do. Now go get clean. I'd like to eat with a gentleman," she teases.

Her words bring a smirk to my face. I turn to head for the bathroom when I feel her hand on my wrist. Before I realize what's happening we're face to face. I'm helpless. She looks right into me with her big green eyes.

"Your breath is much better now that there's no alcohol on it." She sticks her tongue out playfully, releasing my wrist and turning back to the kitchen.

"Wait, Maraye." I say, feeling my chest burn with desire.

"Yeah?" she asks, turning toward me.

"I missed you."

Her lips form a small 'o' shape and her eyes widen. Her look is priceless.

Glancing back one last time, I shut the door to the bathroom and begin to undress. My words start to catch up with my mind as I pull my shirt over my head. I'm shaking and I know what's coming. The nausea drives its fingers into my veins. I collapse onto the bathroom floor and pull myself into the shower still half dressed. My legs shake and I try to stand but I can't stop the shaking. I just slip forward on my knees and vomit above the shower drain. I vomit until my ribs hurt and try to stand once more.

As I'm halfway on my feet I dry heave and slip forward. My head collides with the neck of the tub faucet and I bellow as it scrapes the edge of my scalp. I just curl up and laugh in exasperation as I watch bright red blood drip onto the enamel and flow into the drain.

"She is never coming back," I whisper to myself. "She's never coming back, she's never coming back." The worse the withdrawal becomes, the more I think of losing Maraye, the same way that I lost Lenai. My legs tremble and twitch, banging against the tub wall.

Lenai's last words to me echo through my skull. "Just trust me," she whispered.

"I trusted you!" I scream over and over. "I trusted you! I trusted you! I trusted you!"

I don't know what happens exactly but I'm vaguely aware of the bright lights above me. I hear myself screaming but I can't regain control of my voice. Everything is darkness. I've lost control of my head. I hear screeching tires and metal scraping pavement. The pain that has begun to fade rises again. It endures.

The sound of Maraye's voice and the abrasive hot water bring me back from the abyss. I don't realize I'm speaking at first until the words are out.

"Maraye ... Don't go," I whimper. "Please, don't go. You'll never come back."

She wraps my arm around her waist, helping me to my feet. "I'll always come back," She whispers. "I'm right here. Come on, I won't leave you. I'll run a bath. You just get undressed. I won't look. I'll sit with you. Is that ok?"

"Okay, you think it'll help? I can't breathe."

"Yes, just try to breathe, and get your clothes off. You need to soak and get clean. I'll throw your clothes in the wash. I'll just sit here with you to make sure you're safe, okay?"

True to her word Maraye turns away as I remove the remainder of my clothes and step into the warm bubbly water. I'm feeling much better and the hot water puts my body at ease.

"I'm sorry, Maraye. I think the episode or whatever it was has passed."

"You sure?" she asks, turning around. Her face is full of concern and she blushes a bit, staring at my bare chest. Her eyes move down to my exposed belly button.

"Yeah, I'm sure. I wasn't expecting that. Is that normal?"

"I don't know," she shrugs. "It scared me half to death. I had to use my bobby pin to get the door open. You were yelling and flailing around. Your forehead has a little nick but it's not bleeding now. Are you sure you're ok?"

"Yeah, I'm fine. I feel normal now," I tell her.

"Good. I'll be right back."

I relax and breathe deep, watching her stand and walk out of the bathroom. The steam from the water clouds the bathroom mirrors. My nostrils flare and I sigh deeply, happy that the attack is over. Maraye walks back into the bathroom. I watch as she switches the light off. I hear the click of a lighter as she lights a few candles.

"What are you doing?" I ask. I'm confused but grateful that there is less light to shed on my skin.

"I didn't want the light to give you a head ache. I thought this might help."

She's changed into abnormally low-cut pajama shorts and a white skin-tight tank top. She drops down onto her knees and rests her forearms on the edge of the bathtub.

"Can I tell you something, Maraye?"

"Sure," she says, dodging the bubbles I blow toward her.

"I'm kind of nervous that you're dressed like that while I'm sitting nude, covered only by a few inches of bubbles."

Before I even register what's happening, I can feel the blood rushing toward my lower half. She bites her lip seductively and lifts her right leg into the tub. Warm water splashes out of the tub onto the floor.

"What the fuck are you doing?" I try to lift myself up in horror but I collide with her legs and hips. I fall backward helplessly. She's squealing and laughing loudly.

"You know if you're so self-conscious about me seeing you naked, I'd stop moving if I were you." Her laughter echoes in the tiny bathroom. She slides backward, resting her back on the far side of the tub. Her legs cross and her feet rest on my chest.

"Seriously, Maraye ... what the hell? I'm sick, remember?" I know I'm protesting in vain. It's a half-hearted protest, anyway.

"I'm making you feel better," she says. "Now, be a good boy and relax."

I laugh loudly and I cover my privates with my hands self-consciously.

"You're insane."

She just smiles at me and playfully prods at my nose with her foot. I grin and grab hold, pretending to bite it. We laugh and splash one another. I just stare at her for a moment in silence while my eyes track the part of her body still exposed above the water. I nearly jump out of the tub.

"Maraye, I don't know how to say this but I can see your breasts through your shirt." I don't think I've ever desired any one as much as I want her right now. I'm still very much a normal human man. Her breasts are irresistible. They're creamy white and perky.

"Oh, look at that," she whispers, feigning surprise. "Well ..." She continues. "I told you I was going to make you feel better." She looks at me for approval.

"You're perfect, Maraye. I mean that."

I remember back to the last time I made love to a woman. It was the last night I spent with Lenai and I remember the consequences of my lack of control. My looks must betray my thoughts because she catches on to them.

"Are you thinking of Lenai?" she asks, sliding her foot down my chest onto my stomach.

"Yes," I reply honestly. "It was my fault, wasn't it? She wouldn't have been where she was when she collapsed, if not for me. She might still be alive if it weren't for me ... if I had controlled my desire."

Maraye moves so quickly that I jump from the shock. Her legs wrap around my waist, and she pulls herself toward me. She places her hands on my shoulders and leans in close to my face.

"It wasn't your fault. What happened, just happened ... that's how it went, Emmett. You've got to let go. That it's your fault is just a lie you tell yourself. I think you're just afraid." The tip of her nose is pressed to mine. Her hands are clutching the sides of my head.

"Maraye, I want you. I want you very much."

"Oh, I can feel that," she says, grinning and glancing down into the water.

"Holy God! I'm sorry!"

We're laughing so hard that we both cry. We continue on and I hold my ribs when they begin to hurt.

"Don't look at me! I'm only a man!" I shout defensively.

"No!" Maraye screams between laughs. "I'm so flattered!"

"I have never been so embarrassed in my life," I tell her, my head bowed in shame.

"Oh please, it was bound to happen. At least I don't have to wonder if you want me anymore."

"You'll never have to wonder," I say, staring at her, trying to avoid her chest.

"Good," she replies, moving toward me, spitting water into my face.

"Shit, Maraye ..."

It's too late. My head is over the side of the bath and I'm vomiting before I can warn her. I hear her laugh and feel her stand to exit the tub.

"It's okay, Emmett. You'll be fine. Come on," she says, tossing me a towel.

She helps me into bed. She promises that she'll stay with me. I am filled with guilt as she cleans up my mess. Several times in the next few hours she changes the sheets as I soak them in sweat. I look up at her as she pulls the sheets over me, unsure of how much time I've been here.

"Emmett," she says, gently patting my chest. "I looked online. This is definitely withdrawal. Just hang in there and breathe. I'll get some water. We'll get through this."

Over and over Maraye pulls me back from the abyss. It comes in waves, calming and then roaring. I whisper to her that I want to die rather than endure this any longer. My head hasn't stopped pounding and I can't eat.

The restless leg syndrome makes it impossible to sleep and when I do finally pass out from exhaustion, the dreams are like hell. I can't move even when I become aware that I'm dreaming. I can't open my eyes to make the nightmares stop.

Maraye never leaves my side. She keeps wet rags on my forehead and brings me water. Jack periodically stops in to check on us. He's kind and his words are affirming.

"I know it hurts but it'll be worth it. Hang in there," he tells me.

Whatever strength I have, I draw from Maraye. I sweat and shake, on the verge of hysterics. Everything I see is a kind of darkness. The unceasing delusions and nightmares rage on and on. She whispers in my ear and squeezes my palms in hers. When night falls and the pain grows, she reads to me. The sound of her voice pulls and pulls, keeping me steady.

She speaks in a whisper, "Tiger got to hunt, bird got to fly; Man got to sit and wonder, 'Why, why, why?' Tiger got to sleep, bird got to land; Man got to tell himself he understand."

"I won't leave you," she assures me as I shake and shout into the pillows.

I move in and out of consciousness but notice that Maraye speaks to me when she thinks I'm sleeping. Finally, after the third day, the pain begins to recede. The nightmares continue. I start to lose control of my mind and emotions so I stop speaking entirely. I keep remembering the last night I spent with Lenai. It's fresh as ever. I hear her voice in my mind, clear as the night she died. I look out the window and see it clearly, as though projected on a movie screen.

"Emmett," she said that night. "I need to get sleep before biology tomorrow." I didn't want her to go. I smiled and charmed her into staying with me. I insisted that I could do her homework for her. She stayed with me a little longer.

"You'll come back to me?" I asked as she left, early in the morning hours.

She smiled as she replied, "Yes love, I'll see you tonight." She kissed my lips softly and walked out the door.

I never saw her alive again.

When the self-degradation ceases and I exit my memory, it's clear that I should stop blaming myself. I decide that I should choose to stop but that I'm not there yet. I might not ever be. It's the third night since the withdrawal began.

Maraye looks exhausted. I wake in the night to find her asleep. Outside, rain is tapping on the bedroom window. Somehow I manage to walk to the bathroom. My legs are weak. I feel like I've never used them.

In the warmth of the shower I feel my strength start to return. My thoughts begin to calm, moving to Maraye and away from

Lenai. I want to damn her memory for what it's done to me. I want to damn myself for what I'm afraid I'll do to Maraye.

It's difficult to live with my thoughts, coupled with the pain of withdrawal and detox. If not for the girl asleep in the other room, I'm not sure where I'd be. I'm beginning to think I'm nothing without my fear. The solution to my constant worry eludes me for now.

I'm reborn in the shower. Emerging strong and energetic, I make my way to the kitchen and look for food. It's four in the morning when I return to my bedroom. Maraye is still sleeping like an infant. I pick her up from the chair beside the bed and place her on the mattress. She smiles and pulls the covers over her. It's nice to care for someone else. In fact, I like it a lot.

The burning in my gut returns as I lie down next to her, keeping a healthy distance. Maraye inches closer and places her head on my ribs. The war begins. I run my fingers down her neck, close my eyes and squeeze the sheets in my hand. Maraye moves her hand to my stomach and I'm calmed, rendered paralytic.

Staring out the window to my right I see the woods are quiet and still in the cold rain. It feels like they have a consciousness to them. I think I could just talk through the gray mist and the trees would nod in understanding. Maraye sleeps calmly by my side. The forest life is nice.

Feeling Maraye breathing softly on my ribs, I begin to realize that this life could possibly sustain my will to live. I can't shake the feeling that this may have come to pass much sooner if I had been sober. I think a part of my brain was sleeping under anesthesia from the alcohol and it's awake at last.

Our peaceful reverie and rest continues for a few hours. I stir when I feel Maraye shaking me awake. "Emmett, wake up. Please wake up." I can hear that something is wrong in the way her voice trembles.

"I'm up. What's wrong? Are you okay?" I ask. I'm so groggy that my eyes are refusing to open.

"It's my grandpa. He called me. He's in the hospital. We have to go."

"Shit. Okay, let's go. I'll get dressed."

Her eyes are full of worry as I hurry to get dressed. We don't know what's wrong but I can't ignore the nagging in my head that God has played another joke on me. I resist the urge to fume in anger for Maraye's sake. She looks far more fearful than I feel.

In the car she squeezes my hand as she drives. I'm nauseated. I want to run and never look back but I stay strong for her. This cements the feeling of peril I feel about caring for others, given that any moment a phone call can crush all of that.

"It's going to be okay." I don't think my words are any more comforting to Maraye than they are to me, but I don't know what else to do while she drives.

The hospital is old and small. The emergency area smells like mildew as we pass through on our way to Jack's room. Maraye is panicked and I'm nervous as we arrive. Jack is sleeping when we enter the room. He's hooked up to a saline drip. We wait a few minutes before a young RN comes in to check his vitals. She seems glad to see us.

"Hi," she says, wrapping a blood pressure cuff around his arm. "Are you his family?"

"Yes," Maraye says. "He's my grandpa. What's going on?" The nurse purses her lips nervously and sits in a chair across from Maraye.

"Your grandfather had a heart attack last night while he was on his way home. He was lucky a sheriff's deputy found him off the road in a ditch. He's in bad shape. We're not sure but a spasm in his coronary artery may have caused the attack. He's on oxygen; he was barely breathing when he got here."

Maraye's cheeks are dripping tears. "What can you do?" she asks.

The nurse crosses her legs and leans forward. She gives Maraye the kind of look that a mother would give an upset child. "Sweetheart, the doctor has us running tests, and he'll be in to talk with you in a little while."

"Thank you …" Maraye says weakly, looking back at Jack.

"Just hit the button if you need anything."

"Emmett, I'm afraid," Maraye whispers when the nurse leaves. "You won't leave me?" She's begging for help with her eyes. Help I can't offer.

"It'll be okay," I lie. "We'll get through this and everything will be alright."

She crosses the room and curls up in the chair next to me, placing her head in my lap. "I'd be lost without you, Emmett."

I'm afraid for her. Seeing Jack frail and weak in that bed is like looking in a mirror at my own grandpa. I feel drier than a desert sitting here contemplating the death of someone I care about again. The room is silent as a monastery.

When Jack wakes up he's happy to see us. Maraye explains that we were together when he called. He seems almost pleased with that explanation. We sit for an hour or so watching television. Eventually I doze off.

"Where's Maraye?" I ask when I wake to find her gone.

"She's running to the house. She went to pick up some of my things," Jack answers.

He coughs a bit and reaches for his plastic water bottle. I move quickly and grab it for him so he doesn't strain himself.

"Can I get you anything?"

"No, I'm fine, thank you. Emmett, can I talk with you while we're alone?" he asks, his face serious.

"Of course," I say, fearful of what's to come.

"Emmett, I'm dying…" He stops before he finishes his thought. "It's strange to hear myself say that," he whispers, full of thoughtfulness.

I want to comfort him but I'm lost.

"Jack …" I don't know what to say and I feel the familiar ill inside me.

"It's alright," he starts, "I'm old and rusty. It's just the way things go." He smiles and looks at me, coughs and pushes down on his morphine drip.

"Emmett?" He asks, smiling at me. "Do you forgive yourself?"

I look away for a moment and think back to the dumpster in Brooklyn. I think of Lenai and I think of Sonya urging me to carry on.

"I … I don't know Jack. I don't know what that means."

"But you feel it don't you? That maybe in all of this tragedy, there's something bigger, demanding it from you."

"Sometimes I feel it," I say.

"I feel it, too," he says, taking my hand. "I call it God." The bed creaks as he pulls himself upright. His voice is weak and his hands are shaking. "Although, I don't think whatever *it* is minds what we call it. I don't think that it's a coincidence that you came here to us. I don't think you realize how important you are to Maraye. She's going to need you, the way you need her. I see it when you look at her. And I know you're hurt bad, son. It probably even hurts for you to care about other people. But I know you need each other to get through all the things to come."

He starts coughing again but continues when the fit recedes.

"I need you," he tells me. "I know it's a lot to ask. But I need to believe you'll take care of her when I'm gone."

I know where he's going with this and it's breaking me, filling me with anger. I squeeze my palms with my fingernails but remain calm.

"Jack, I can't be responsible for anyone."

I do my best not to sound angry but I'm not convinced that I conceal it. He smiles at me with moist eyes. I can see that he's tired. It doesn't matter how I spin it; it all feels like a betrayal of Lenai. If I stay here with Maraye, it's as though Lenai never meant a thing to me. It's as though she were a cheap trinket that I lost. It'll be like I've merely shrugged my shoulders and carried on. Did I ever really love her? My anger and guilt continues to swell and swell as Jack speaks.

"I know it's not fair of me to ask you this. I know you're still struggling and suffering through your own grief but we need you. Maraye needs you and I know you care for her. I know she might be the only reason you've stuck around at all. I believe you can help each other."

"What do I do?"

He's looking at me but I feel as though he's looking past me at something unseen. "Emmett, it's up to you to figure that out. But all of this means something." He coughs again, harder this time. "I know it does. The two of you need to walk through the fire together from now on. You can't get through life alone, Emmett."

Burying my face in my hands, the harsh reality confronts me. I've been tricked into living with my suffering. It's not in me to abandon Maraye. Beyond that, I'm beginning to feel affection for her as strong as I felt for Lenai. The reality of it all sets the guilt on fire. And so I add anger to the spectral fire of guilt and grief.

"You've been nothing but good to me. I'll look after her the best that I can." The pain of Jack's imminent demise tugs and pulls at me but I maintain my composure.

"You're a good man, Emmett," he says.

We spend all our time at Jack's bedside for the next few weeks. He mostly sleeps. He's much weaker than usual so I help him walk through the hallway to prevent blood clots. It's strange but I find myself enjoying my time at the hospital.

It's nice to be in Jack and Maraye's world. It almost feels like a family. They sit and whisper and laugh with one another. Some nights I stay with Maraye. I sleep in the small sleeper against the window of the room.

Tonight I can't sleep. I'm lost in the past as usual staring at the television. Jack's voice sounds from a few feet away.

"What's keeping you awake, Emmett?" He pulls himself up and pushes down on the button to raise his bed.

"I'm not sure …" I lie. Jack's hand grasps mine as I hand him a cup of water.

"Whatever it is, you've got to forgive yourself."

"That's the second time you've told me that. You know what's weird? I saw that phrase spray painted on a dumpster once," I tell him.

"Did you?" he asks.

"I did. Isn't that funny?"

"Yes, I should think so." He smiles. "You really loved them, didn't you?" His face falls and he stares at me. "The people you lost? The girl?"

"I still do."

"Of course," he says apologetically. "I miss my wife. But I was fortunate, wasn't I? We had a life together, the two of us. My grief is very different from yours. You must have been full of hope and dreams. I am sorry for you, my boy."

"That's alright. I'm over it."

"Can you even remember the last night you slept without stirring?" he asks knowingly.

"No, I guess not."

"Good, you're still human." He winks at me but his face still looks sad.

"Some nights I wish I wasn't," I confess.

"You're very brave. You're brave for trying to make sense of all this instead of just giving in to the bad. Most men just succumb to the dark."

"I've given in many times."

"But you're still fighting. You owe it to the people who love you to keep fighting."

"Is it worth it? Do you have regrets?" I ask, wanting to know his thoughts on a long life.

"Oh yes," he smiles. "What an adventure this has been. Every mistake and triumph and every painful memory was worth it. The world needs people like you and Maraye in it. It needs people who can think well."

"If I could think well, I wouldn't be in this mess," I say bitterly.

"It's precisely because you think well that you are in this mess," he counters. "Being able to love and think is what this is all about. It's no good if you can't do both. Look at Jesus…"

"Jack …" I'm in no mood for a sermon.

"I know … I know …" He says. "You don't have to think anything of him or God. That's not what I'm saying. All I'm saying is that he seemed to love well enough to inspire a lot of people. And his teachings aren't bad either, even if people abuse them."

"Fair enough," I concede.

"Just try to get some sleep. You make an old man like me worry."

"Alright," I say. "Goodnight."

"Goodnight, son."

Jack died this morning. It's Friday. We lost him in his sleep. The attending nurse asks us to leave the room, consults with the floor doctor and she confirms the time of death. She's

Russian and her accent is thick. We can't understand much of her condolence but it's a nice gesture.

Maraye cries but remains reserved. She handles everything that follows with grace. She's prepared herself for this moment. When we go back to her house she loses her composure. There isn't anything I could have done to brace her. His departure has turned her into a sleepless zombie.

"I wasn't ready," she tells me as we sit on her small twin bed. I run my hands over the well-kept purple comforter. I am hurting over Jack's death but I don't feel the grief that Maraye is feeling. There's only so much you can feel for a person you hardly know.

"Nothing can prepare you for losing someone you love. All we can do is roll with the punches," I tell her.

"How did you do it?" she asks. "How did you live alone after Lenai? If I didn't have you with me, I don't know what I'd do." I feel damp warmth on my shoulder from where she's crying.

"I didn't do it, Maraye. I checked out."

"Aren't we a pair?" She crosses the room and walks into the bathroom, closing the door softly behind her.

She starts running water in the bathtub but I can still hear her sobs.

Jack's service is small but eloquent. The funeral parlor is covered in black and red ornaments. Strangers console Maraye with kind words and nice stories. The air is somewhat warm and humid in the evening as the service wraps up. I'm asked to say a few words by the kind pastor conducting the service. My hands shake while I walk to the podium next to his coffin.

"Jack was all the things a man should be," I say. The mourners are staring up at me. "He took me in as his own. I'm just an orphan stranger and he cared for me. I had the honor of spending his remaining days with him. I'm not sure what to say or how to articulate the goodness I felt in him. He was a man who overcame his demons, an inspiration to me."

I pause for a moment and look beyond the crowd. I feel like an impostor, having hardly known Jack.

"I didn't know him very well but he kept watch over me. It's an immense act of love to care for someone you don't know the way that he did. We'd all do well to take notes from his life. I hope we see him on the other side."

Later, after he's lowered into the ground, Maraye and I wait. She asks me to stay with her while she greets and accepts more condolences from people who knew Jack.

Hours later, we are finally alone at the marina. Maraye cries on my shoulder until the rain stops and then continues to cry. I'm mostly silent. I don't know how to comfort a grieving person. So we just sit here staring out at the water. We're just together.

She stays with me for over a week. I help her sort out the mundane, yet painful details that accompany the death of a loved one. She rarely speaks.

Today we're sitting in Jack's old pontoon boat next to the marina. After a while she breaks the silence. She smiles and hands me a root beer.

"He told me to look after you, ya know. I don't know how to take care of you, Emmett, but I love you. You don't have to say anything back. I just want to tell you I love you and I'm glad you're here with me. I'm glad you came back to me."

She turns and looks at me, smiling and attempting to read my reaction. In a fit of madness I sweep her up into my arms, spilling our sodas. I start running, right to the edge of the marina. She screams as I run right off the ledge and into the dark water.

The cold water causes us to scream in pain. I'm laughing and yelling.

"What the hell, Emmett!" Maraye screams through the laughter. She's squeezing my body as tight as she can in the cold water. Her arms are wrapped around my neck, her lips inches from my own. Her body is trembling from the shock.

"Just have fun with me. I never have fun, Maraye!" Her smile is all that I need. More than anything I just want to make her smile and feel less alone in this mess. Tonight, for Jack, we're just young and happy. Tonight the whole forest hears our bones crack in the icy water.

"This was a horrible idea!" I yell and struggle to swim toward the shore. "Let's get the hell out of here."

Back in the cabin we strip down out of our wet clothes while I start a fire. Inadvertently, I see more of Maraye's skin than I intend to. The burning in my gut makes me nervous but I hold it at bay. Something bright burns inside of us. We lay together on the couch, her head on my stomach. Her skin is covered only by a small nightgown. It's a thin material and presses against her tightly. I see all of her curves and her erect nipples press against the cloth. She doesn't seem to care.

"You're crazy, you know that? I mean it; I'm going to get sick." I look down and smile at her. She's beauty incarnate: gentle and lovely, a stark contrast to my wrecked mind. It takes all my self-control to keep my hands to myself. I fight it but I imagine sliding my hands up her ribs and wrapping my arms around her back before pulling her close.

"Emmett," she says. "Do you think he can see us from some place right now?"

"I don't know," I whisper back. "I imagine if he can he's smiling. He made me promise to watch after you, as well. I'm glad he did, even though it's a lot to ask. I'm afraid of responsibility."

"I'm glad he asked you," she says. "He would have liked to see you smile like this. He was still looking out for me, even when he should have been looking after himself."

"Do you think we'll see them again? In another life or something?"

"I don't know," I say. "I'd like to think that all of this means something. But I don't have conclusive evidence one way or the other."

I pause before I start rambling. I stand and walk to the table and pull out one of the daisies that Maraye is keeping in a vase. She smiles as I stroke her hair to place the flower in it.

"You sure live like it means something, Emmett. Even if you don't feel like it does. You care so much. I don't know what any of this means but this moment is nice."

"Yes," I say. "It is nice."

And so it goes. We drift to sleep, warm and safe.

Morning comes and drags us back to reality. We spend a few days dealing with Jack's attorney and legal matters. Neither of us is comfortable benefiting from the death of a loved one. The process is painful and awkward.

The ironic joke continues as Maraye and I learn we are both beneficiaries in a large inheritance. The cabin I was renting now belongs to me. Maraye has inherited a few hundred thousand dollars in life insurance claims and savings. Jack was apparently preparing for his departure since the death of his wife, not wanting to leave Maraye stranded.

She keeps her job at Maggie's. We decide to hold off on all of our decision-making. I'm still trying to work things out, my remorse slowly creeping its way back. I don't know what do when it hits hard one night. I spend the night in my room staring at my straight razor as Maraye sleeps. The distraction of Jack's death has worn off and the guilt and suffering have returned with a vengeance. I don't know what to do and I hide it from Maraye. I'm not sure where it came from but I just lie against the wall, suffering. Lenai's memory is here and I am entirely beset by it.

The worry of my inability to love keeps me awake. I remember Josef telling me that we need just one person to love and be loved by to make it in this life. I can't love Maraye the way she deserves. I don't think I can love her the way she needs me to love her. I'm strangled by guilt when it occurs to me that a few days have gone by without a thought of Lenai. I cry silently with my hands over my head.

I'm not sure why any of this is happening but tonight I feel like I don't want to let myself recover from Lenai's death. It feels like a betrayal. But Maraye, this place and that elemental force inside of me that I can't name push me toward recovery.

I fall asleep and wake to Maraye and the reality of life. We move through another day together. I'm desperately in love with the conversations we have at night. We drink hot tea and sit together, reading and playing chess in front of the warm fire.

We sleep and wake up for several weeks and all the while, I silently struggle with the weight of my guilt while I help Maraye continue to deal with Jack's affairs.

She sells his land piece by piece and puts the house up for sale as well. It's far too much for her to manage alone. She sleeps at the cabin with me every night. I don't blame her and I certainly don't mind the company. When we return to her house to clear her stuff out and clean, I can see that she looks at it the same way I viewed my apartment in Brooklyn after Lenai died. The things that made it her home are gone now.

Tonight we return to the cabin exhausted from trashing and scrapping a few of the work sheds on Jack's farm.

"Emmett," Maraye says, pulling up my shirt and revealing my ribs. "How did you get that scar?" I look down at the scar above my ribs. It's a few inches long.

"Do you want the truth?" I ask her as I step into my time machine.

"Yes."

"I drove my car into a median on the highway while I was driving to Baltimore for Lenai's funeral."

"Did you fall asleep or something? That's awful."

At first I consider lying to her but I don't. "No," I tell her. "I didn't want to live anymore. Obviously my plan didn't work out."

Maraye stands and moves toward me. Her arms are around my neck, her head on my chest. I stretch out my arms behind her, unsure how to carry myself. Slowly I move my hand up her back, along her arm and move her hair through my fingers. The stark black of her hair contrasts my pale white fingers.

"You're too good of a man to go before your time, Emmett." Her breath warms my chest.

"Maraye, I'm a wrecked monster of a person. If you could see my insides ..." I pause. I don't know how to tell her how much more hopeless Jack's death makes me feel.

"If you knew how I feel, Maraye, if you could feel it ..." I try in vain to explain.

"How do you feel?" she asks, pulling me closer, looking up into my eyes. "You've seemed distant lately." Her words pull me from my time machine. They push the harsh circumstances of reality into view. I am getting worse.

I freeze as her hands move up my ribs to my shoulders, and pull on the collar of my shirt. Her lips press against mine; I grit my teeth and wrap my hands around her waist pulling her closer. I just rest in the moment and dissolve into her touch. After a moment I look beyond her while resting my head on her shoulder.

I am afraid. I am conflicted.

"Let's just walk together," I tell her. I kiss her once more and graze her cheek with my bottom lip, pressing my body against her.

"Alright," she breathes back.

We walk down through the familiar poppies toward the shoreline. It's bitter cold but my thermal keeps me comfortable.

"I don't know what to do, Maraye. I'm afraid and I'm torn to pieces. It's making me sick. It's coming back again. The way it was before."

"What do you mean?" she asks, wrapping her arm in my mine. I look over to her, tears swelling in my eyes.

"I feel like I just cheated on Lenai with you." She moves to pull away but I hold her firmly, turning her to meet my eyes. Hers are full of tears. "Maraye, please don't. It's how I feel. It scares me."

"She isn't here, Emmett. She's not coming back."

"I know. What do I do? It's eating me alive. And Jack's gone now ..."

"Why can't you just be here with me? I'm right here. I'm yours if you want me. Can't you just let go? We can be happy together, the two of us." Her words break whatever's left in me to break.

"I do want you, Maraye, so much more than I let on. I'm not whole. It's like I belong to her. I'm in fucking pieces."

"Emmett, you throw the good out with the bad. What is it you find so appealing about letting yourself suffer? I've seen you with me. You can be happy if you choose to be. You can let yourself be happy."

"I didn't choose any of this. What's the point in living aimlessly? I have no purpose and I can't feel like I did before when I was completely happy. How do I get it back?"

"We can rest in each other, Emmett. We have a choice. We're not the things we've lost, not the people left behind in memory."

In moments it feels as though it would be incredibly simple just to sink into Maraye completely. But I can't hold her to me when I know how unstable I am. I can't risk her happiness in my condition.

"You don't want to let yourself love like that again, do you?"

I stop walking and look closely at her.

"Maybe I'm afraid," I say. "But mostly I don't want you to end up like me. I'm such a mess. I go back and forth all the time. I could destroy you."

"That's my choice. You shouldn't make it for me."

The moon seems so close it could eavesdrop. The weight of life's trickery crushes down on me. Two lovers separated by silly misfortunes. I feel like giving in and letting go. I look down toward the marina and remember my drunken attempt at suicide by drowning. I close my eyes, not wanting phantom Lenai to visit me. I'm so tired of the fear.

"I don't know how to put things back together, Maraye. This is why people take medication."

She takes my hand in hers, softly kisses it, sending chills through my bones. "I'll wait for you to figure it out."

"Why? Can't you hear what I'm saying?" I ask, frustrated and angry now. "I'm not a full person anymore. You're just getting pieces of me."

She looks at me unaffected by my words. "I love you, Emmett."

I'm silent as she turns and walks back to the cabin. Staring at the sky I walk to the end of the marina and sit down. My thoughts slowly come and go as I stare blankly out at the calm water.

The irony isn't lost on me. My self-imposed exile couldn't have gone more awry if I'd planned it. A cold wind drifts over me. The noiseless woods shine on the surface of the lake. I'm completely unsure what to do with my past. I want to leave but I can't. I want to escape before I'm trapped here. I'm attached to Maraye and I made a promise to Jack. What sort of nihilist am I anyway, despairing over promises I made to a man who is now buried in the earth?

I think Jack's death must have set this in motion. It must have reminded me of the futility of love and attachment. All of the grief drifts back over me. I punch the earth beneath me. I've turned my back on Lenai. I tell myself that Maraye will be fine if I run now. She has money and she'll recover, find someone new. Someone intact. Even as I tell myself this, I don't believe it.

When I return to the cabin, Maraye is asleep on a chair at the kitchen table. Slowly I walk over and sit next to her. She brings a peace, a sense of home to this cabin that was never here before her arrival. I've grown complacent being warm with her, placing my questions and imponderables on the backburner.

My thoughts return to my grandfather's razor. My entire purpose was centered on suicide. I could do it quickly before all of the unending questions make their way back to surface and Maraye watches me fall apart any more than I already have. What am I to make of my life now that its urgency is receding? The anger surges as I softly pick up Maraye's tiny frame and carry her to the couch. She blinks at me as I sit down, resting her head on my lap. I close my eyes to suppress the saline from leaking but it breaks through. How can I make the happiness she brings me stay for good?

I don't know.

In the back of my mind I hear the acoustic piano keys and a xylophone playing my make-believe composition. The notes come and go. I can't keep my promise to Jack with plans for suicide roaming through my mind. I don't know how to keep Maraye safe and whole. Do I just stay here in my torment and suffering? It seems like the right thing to do but I'm not sure I can sustain the will to live. Surely Maraye will begin to notice that I'm back to my old self.

I grit my teeth, wanting to lash out at God. If God does exist, I surely hate it for doing this to me. I can't leave Maraye here with Jack gone. I've been tricked and trapped and roped into living a life of suffering and futility. I don't think I have faith in a God but this seems almost too cruel to be mere chance. I rebuke the thought and tell myself that this is just the way it goes. Some God is laughing somewhere, dangling questions without answers in front of me.

"Emmett …" Maraye says, stirring on my lap. "Go away with me. Let's go away from here for a while."

"What do you mean?" I ask. Her hand reaches up and cradles my neck.

"Let's go somewhere far away."

"What are you running away from life like me now?"

"No," she says, sitting up. "I just want to go somewhere lovely with you. I want to share something nice with you."

"Where do you want to go?"

"I'll surprise you. How 'bout that?"

"That sounds fine. Are you sure?"

"Yes, I'm sure. I need a change of scenery. Just come with me. After that, you can leave if you need to go. I'll let you go." She leans in and kisses me hard. I return her fervor and press my thumbs into her hips.

My mind expands, then collapses, then expands again. "Maraye …" I say, pulling myself away.

"Let's sleep," she says, motioning for me to lie next to her. I move slowly and pull her body close to mine. It's like moving toward the sun. I want her close to me, keeping me warm.

For a while I set my mind on slipping away in the middle of the night. I'm not sure I have the strength to leave and I think of it for hours. Eventually I dismiss the idea and drift to sleep.

I know what I want. I want to go with her. I want to have one last moment with her and then I want to end myself. I want to be rid of myself at last. I don't want to have to deal with responsibility and fear and pain anymore. I want to be gone for good.

CHAPTER 10

I've learned that there are many unknowable things in this life. It seems to me the majority of the important things are unknowable. Most people spend their lives fleeing the imponderables, and rightly so. I'm too stupid now to turn and walk away. I've let them drive me mad. I've allowed them to gain a hold and strangle me. I'm convinced this is the fate of all who love.

The great fools: lovers.

I'm sitting here, a great fool, in an Airbus A380 cruising at thirty thousand feet on my way to Alaska. Maraye woke me yesterday morning and rushed me into a packing fury. She didn't reveal our destination until we arrived at the airport and I figured it out.

"Grandpa always wanted to see Alaska." She tells me as she trips over her bag. I grab her arm to steady. She smiles at me. "Thanks."

She's been cheerful but I can sense an undertone of somberness. It's a seven-hour flight from Memphis to Anchorage. I can't take my eyes off of her. In the back of my mind I know these are the last days we'll spend together and I want to focus on making her happy. She notices the extra attention and smiles at me. I find her rose colored knuckles oddly attractive. My fingers trace the grooves up to her fingertips while she clutches my hand. I've given up trying to resist her and I just give in to my desire, knowing what's to come. When I kill myself I want to believe that I'll cease to be at all so I can't remember any of this.

I mark her appearance in my memory, just on the off chance that I carry it with me into some other life after I've gone. She's wearing blue tights and a blue dress garbed with yellow flowers. Her lips are adorned with red lipstick, not light but not vibrant. Her black bangs are down to her eyebrows and her hair is pulled into a ponytail. She is breathtaking. Nothing marks me as deeply as the green in her eyes.

Halfway through the flight I drift off into dreams of Lenai. She approaches me in the woods. I recognize the familiar oaks of Paris. She moves toward me.

"Emmett ..." she breathes. The sound of her voice shakes me. I'd nearly forgotten the way it shook me. "Come on, take a walk with me." She takes my hand and leads me through the thick.

I try to speak but nothing happens.

"What are you doing here, Emmett?" I don't understand her question. I'm confused. I'm lost. I can hear the branches cracking under our feet. "You can't hold a ghost," she tells me as we walk into the clearing on the shore of the lake. I see my lifeless body among the weeds before I wake.

I try and cover my face. I pull myself together and look over at Maraye. She's staring at me. "Nightmare?" she asks.

"I don't know ..." I lie. "I can't remember ..."

"You were mumbling. You're okay?"

"Yes, everything's alright," I say, closing my eyes. All of this deception is getting old.

"Emmett ..." Maraye says, breaking my focus. "If someone created us, do you think something was lost before us?"

I'm tired of talking about death but I respond anyway, hiding my irritation. "What are you talking about?"

"Some religions hold the idea that death is an act of creation. If we were created, what died and broke God's heart? What did God lose? Do you think God was trying to replace something it lost?"

"I don't know," I say, my interest growing. "Maybe he was heartbroken over Satan abandoning him or betraying him or whatever happened."

"Yes, I imagine he loved him at some point," She says thoughtfully.

"What are you getting at?"

"Nothing," she says. "I just think it's interesting that even God has loved and lost. I guess it was inevitable. Real love is about choices. There's always a choice or it wouldn't be love, right?"

"Real love is about fools being fools," I say. She sits silent looking at me, trying to hide her hurt.

Consciously, I push the dream to the back of my mind and focus on Maraye. I forget about the other passengers and crying babies until the end of the flight drags me back to reality. She stays close to me, clutching my arm, as we make our way through the terminal to pick up our baggage. Eventually we exit the terminal and move toward the rental car pickup area.

Maraye gasps and I turn to see her covering her mouth with her hand. "Those are some mountains," she says, pointing at the peaks around us and smiling.

I look at the beauty around us. We're here and that means I'm nearly out of time. I can feel the sickness spreading inside of me. The guilt and grief is winning out.

This is a nice place to die.

We spend a few days in the city of Anchorage. It's a beautiful city. We explore the parks. I take Maraye bird watching and point out the different species. While sitting near a stream we watch an osprey swoop down and snatch a salmon. Each night

Maraye is harder to resist. I want to make love to her so badly and I can see that she wants me but she restrains herself.

The Alaska Zoo is nice. I take pictures of Maraye posing in front of snow leopards, tigers and Tibetan yaks. Afterward we hike to the base of Mt.Williwaw and have a picnic. It's here that I stop long enough to truly admire the beauty of this place. It's undeveloped and mostly unpopulated. Humans haven't screwed it up yet.

On the sixth day we leave our hotel behind and head into the wilderness. I'm silent on the ride.

We drive nearly 45 minutes outside of Anchorage to a place called Palmer. Maraye arranged for us to stay in a small rental house. It's in the Matanuska Valley on the very edge of the Matanuska River. It's a breathtaking sight to behold. The small house resembles an upscale loft barn with a bedroom and bathroom. It's warm and comforting, muted earth tones of brown and green. It's a welcome refuge amidst the wild surrounding us.

Maraye is ecstatic. "Isn't it beautiful, Emmett?" she asks, nearly sprinting off into the valley.

I smile and nod. She returns to the cabin and begins to settle in as I slowly make my way down to the shore of the river. It's about a two-foot drop off to the water's edge. I turn and look back to see Maraye moving back and forth through the open door. I feel guilty for what I'm going to do. But guilt is the reason I'm leaving this life behind. Only a little while longer and I'll be set free.

Only a little while longer and I'll be rid of this world: no more war, no more death, no more suffering and no more love lost to circumstances. No more goddamned pain. Maraye approaches and sits beside me, draping her legs over the drop off.

"It's a lovely world," she says.

"It certainly can be," I reply. "It's terminal though, like all things."

"What do you mean?"

"It has a disease. It has humanity and if I'm honest, I don't think it has much time left. We just don't care."

Maraye doesn't respond to me. I'm sure she's tired of my constant pessimism.

"Emmett, I love you." She looks at me full of courage and desire.

"I love you too, Maraye."

The truth comes out. It's too late to mean much of anything but it's nice to confess it. The moment I admitted it to myself I knew that I was too far-gone to continue living. I knew that the guilt had won out the fight. I can't love Maraye and continue to live with the guilt that it brings.

We disregard time. A canopy of quiet moves over us. I can't hide the sorrow in my eyes. She feels it too but doesn't break her hold. I stand to retreat back to the house but she stops me.

"Can we just sit together? Just for a while longer?" she asks, pulling me back down.

"Okay, let's watch the sunset together," I say, knowing it could be my last. We sit silent and afraid, two lovers clinging to unrelenting time. I continue to mark everything she does, her movements and words.

The sun brushes the sky a soft orange. The eagles ride thermals and the wind cuts across our cheeks. We skip rocks on the river. The ripples stir and Maraye snaps pictures of trout gorging on salmon eggs.

Today is a nice day.

We make our way back inside. I run my fingers through my uncombed hair and look over as Maraye emerges from the bedroom wearing a short evening dress. My pulse quickens when I notice the bulk of her legs revealed. Her hair is resting on her shoulders. She nervously twirls her bangs and looks at me. I'm afraid so I walk outside and sit on the hood of our rental car. A few minutes later Maraye joins me.

"If heaven looks like this, it'll be nice. Won't it?" she asks.

"That's what they say," I respond. I smile reluctantly as Maraye's thumb clutches my finger.

"I hope it's just one big open view that goes on forever and I hope we'll just be okay. I hope we'll just breathe deep and know that the worst is all behind us. We won't have to sleep for comfort any more. Maybe we'll just sleep because we can. I hope grandpa's there right now."

She glances over at me, running her hands over her dress. Her green eyes and soft pink lips are a nice kind of forgetfulness.

"Maybe," I say. "At best we'll just cease to be and forget all of this. At worst we'll be stuck singing contemporary Christian worship songs for the rest of eternity, whatever eternity means."

"What about hell?" she asks me as the shadows of the rocks spread over us.

"We're already surrounded by people who aren't getting it right. How can hell be any worse than this?" Her laughter makes me smile.

"It would be nice for my head to be quiet, whenever all this is over. Hell for me would mean having to go on forever trying to understand things that can't be understood."

"I know how to quiet your head, Emmett. You try too hard to make sense of the world. Give it a rest for a while. Dance with me!" She laughs as she pulls me off the hood of the car and I twirl with a half-smile.

We dance for a while with her head on my chest and hands wrapped in my own. The tension mounts when I look into her eyes. She bites down on her lip and breaks the spell, releasing my hands.

"I'll make us some dinner," she says, walking back inside.

I stay here and look out into the brush. Phantom Lenai is standing out on the plain looking in at me.

"Don't worry," I sound in my head, "I'm almost there."

Soon this will all fade into nothingness. Soon I'll cease to be. I sit and think about what it means to die for a while before my thoughts are interrupted.

"Emmett," Maraye says behind me. "It's ready."

We eat quickly. I stare at Maraye from across the table and she returns my look. She makes me think of Jack. It feels like he should be here with us. He was lucky to have died with a measure of grace, feeling complete. In his last days he was with his family. I place my hands over my mouth to hide my shaking jaw.

I can't hold on much longer. I resist the urge to flee from here, get drunk and die in a gutter. I stay because I want these last few hours with Maraye.

"What do you think of all this money we have now?" she asks.

"I think money and things like it distract us from the journey we're on. There are other things going on here. All that crap is irrelevant to me."

"I'm afraid to face those things," she says, looking at me with worried eyes and arched eyebrows.

"You should be," I say. I can hear the harshness in my words.

"You're not afraid?" she asks. I can tell she's trying to overlook my tone and see what I'm feeling.

"Not anymore. Everything I feared has come to pass. What's to be afraid of?" I say, looking away.

"Emmett ... stop thinking like that. You're worrying me. You've seemed off since we've been here. Is everything okay?"

"Everything's alright, Maraye." I offer her a convincing smile to calm her nerves.

"Okay," she says, standing to clean up the kitchen.

"I'll be by the river," I say, making for the door.

"Wait ..." I turn around. She starts moving toward me. "Stay right here with me." My voice breaks when I see the way she's looking at me.

Before I can argue she wraps her hands around my neck and pulls my lips to her. She squeezes the back of my neck tightly and moans slightly as my lips find her neck and move down to her collarbone. She laughs as I lift her up and we fall backward to the table. Our impact sends the plates and silverware across the floor.

Effortlessly I carry her to bed. We move in unison, loving each other with all that we are. The bed frame rattles. The floor shakes beneath us. She moans loudly, clutching the back of my head.

I'm lost in her and I never want to be found. I don't want this to end because I know what will follow. I feel her fingernails cut through my back as she pushes her flesh against mine, harder and harder. I kiss her breasts and palm her hips, moving back and forth. Her body arches in pleasure as we climax together. She shakes through her orgasm, and I join her. After a few moments I collapse beside her. Her tongue finds mine and she continues to tremble in my arms.

"I love you, Emmett."

"I love you, Maraye. I truly do."

I lie still, trying to avoid the inevitable turmoil that is to come.

"You're not going to let me in there, are you?" she asks, tapping my head. Her naked skin rests on mine and she holds herself up on my chest, staring into my eyes.

"You wouldn't like it in there anyway," I say dryly.

"I'm fine with just the parts you let me see," she responds, resting her chin beneath my neck. "I know they're back up again but I live for the moments when you let your barriers down for me."

"I'm sorry, Maraye. I am. I'm sorry I'm such damaged goods."

"It's alright." She rubs her hands over my thighs and across my waist. "We'll put you back together."

"I don't know if there's anything left to put back together."

When I awake later in the night Maraye is still asleep next to me. Her hand rests in mine. I move quickly and silently. I want to finish it before I can feel again. Before I can think about what I'm doing. I dress in the dark and move toward the door. In the doorway I turn to see her as tears pour uninhibited across my face. I can't forgive myself for any of the things I've done, for what I've let happen. I open the door and walk out into the cold.

As I'm walking to the shoreline I feel the memories I'd forgotten return imperceptibly. I see Lenai laughing as we walk down the street in Brooklyn. She looks stunning in a black dress she'd worn for our anniversary dinner. I recall my grandfather sitting with me, explaining the phoenix legend.

"Everyone who lives is a phoenix, Emmett. Remember that," he tells me.

I see Maraye in front of my face, clinging to my neck in the cold water. I see her smiling at me while we're out on the lake. I see her as we make love. I nearly collapse as I recall what giving in to my weakness cost Lenai. I cost Lenai her life and now I offer mine in return.

The cool grass brushes across my legs as I draw near the drop of the river. I drop down and step to the river's edge. The entire world around me is in darkness but I see the scene in color. I see the black water and gold stars reflected. I reach into my pocket and pull out my grandfather's razor. I start to weep, reliving more memories. My lungs nearly collapse as I shove my face into the frigid water. When I emerge I run my hands over my face screaming into the silent night.

"Come back!" I scream, pounding my fists over and over onto the rocks. Blood trickles down my fingers into the river. "I trusted you! I trusted you!"

No one is here to respond to my pleas. I continue pounding my fists. I scream into the water, standing and stumbling, falling back to my knees and weeping. I flail frantically as the razor slips from my fingers. In the shallow water I feel my hand brush it and I pull it back from the black water.

I open the razor and cut across my arm. In my panic I miss the mark and the cut is shallow. It's hardly more than a scratch. Nonetheless, the blood flows and I press the razor back to my wrist. I'm ready to steady myself. I need to focus to cut deep and concisely. Lenai's voice flows through my head and I hesitate. "Trust me, Emmett."

"Why?" I weep to no one. "Why? Why did she die? Why are they all dead?" The silence is infuriating. There is nothing and no one. "You made me love you," I say to Lenai's apparition. "You tricked me."

I glance down to my blood soaked arm. It'll be like falling asleep. It'll be like none of this ever happened at all. None of it will exist. It won't matter. There is no age to come.

I shouldn't be here living like it never happened. I shouldn't fall in love when she's dead. I should be dead in the ground somewhere. I deserve to be alone and forgotten. It was my selfishness that put her in death's sights. It was my love that kept her out of her bed when she should've been warm and safe.

"Kill me!" I scream, banging my head on the rocks. "Kill me! Kill me! Kill me!" Visions of myself waking to Lenai choke me out. I recall my promise to Jack. I think of Maraye back in bed, waiting anxiously for me to return. She'll wait forever. I deserve to die. "Kill me!" I shout at the sky.

I get to my feet and wade deeper into the shallow river. I stumble and fall to my knees and squeeze the razor firmly above my arm. "I'm sorry, Maraye." My scream spreads through the plain as I close my eyes, trying to steady my hand.

"Come on, goddammit." I'm struggling to bring myself to cut.

"Emmett," a voice sounds from behind me. I turn to see Maraye, tears streaming down her cheeks, past her lips and off her chin. She runs to me in the water, grabbing my arm.

"Oh God, Emmett." Her eyes are locked on the blood dripping down my arm. The blood slides over my knuckles off the blade in my palm.

She reaches for my hand, shaking and sobbing uncontrollably.

"Don't!" I say moving the blade over my vein. The grief darts through me. "I'm so sorry, Maraye. I love you."

"Emmett!" she screams hysterically. "I love you. I love you. I love you. Please, stay with me. Don't go. Please, be with me. I'll do anything," she cries. The pain is unbearable.

"Please," she pleads. "Please, don't go."

"I don't know how to live anymore, Maraye. I killed her. It was my fault." I'm barely audible through my sobs. "I can't love you after what I did to her. I don't deserve you. Just let me do this. I have to get away from all of this. I can't be happy with you when I've destroyed her life. It's gone ... love ... goodness ... It's all gone."

"It's never gone," she responds. "Never ... It's right here with us. It's pushing that thing into your skin. Please, Emmett, be with me. I love you."

She's on her knees next to me. She's reaching through the water. I close my eyes and feel her hand wrap around mine pulling on the razor. "Emmett," she says, "You're bleeding. You're hurt." I push hard despite her hand resisting. My resolve is crumbling.

"Please Emmett," she pleads. "You didn't have control over what happened to Lenai but you can control what happens to me right now. I need you. I love you. Don't do this to yourself.

Don't do this to me. Let go, Emmett. Please ..."The sound of her pleas rips me apart. "We can be together. We can help each other through life. Please, Emmett, I can't do this without you. Stay here with me."

I look up at her, trying hard to breath between the sobs. Her hair is matted. Her eyeliner is strewn across her face. She's desperate to save me. Her perfection still stuns me. She has the opportunity I never had with Lenai. She can fight for me.

My body is beginning to go numb. My grip on the razor is weakening. "Maraye, it was my fault. I deserve to die. I deserve this. You don't know me. You don't know who I was. I was on fire. I was happy."

"Emmett, you can let go. You can forgive yourself. You never wanted to hurt anyone. You never meant to hurt anyone. It's a lie, Emmett. You believe a lie. Can't you see the truth? You've done so much good. You've made me whole." She's hysterical now, pulling me out of the water. I half stumble and collapse at the waterline. I can't speak. I just sit with her and sob.

"I have to die, Maraye. I have to make this stop."

I look into the distance and conjure my phantom Lenai. In my mind I plead for forgiveness. But she isn't really there. It isn't real. There is no point in entertaining delusions any longer. It no longer makes her feel close. She's really gone.

"Goodbye," I whisper, dropping the razor and reaching for Maraye.

We don't speak. I cling to her. I push the familiar ghosts to the back of my mind and bid them farewell. I look hard into Maraye's eyes and she returns my gaze.

"I want to live," I whisper.

She moves forward, pressing her head against mine, clutching tighter still. For what seems like days we clutch each other. I feel something change in my thoughts. My fear of the approaching darkness is receding.

Nature sings a lament for us in the form of the wind moving through the grass across the water and sweeping over the mountains. Much like love transcends death and disease, my spirit transcends my anguish and life's futility.

Looking up into her eyes I see everything. I see her eyeliner, her beautiful black eyeliner. "Maraye," I say. "It's so beautiful."

"What is?" She asks.

"Your eyeliner. It's so beautiful."

"I won't let it take you, Emmett." She's shaking and shivering, wiping my arm off to make sure I'm really okay. It's not bleeding now, just a small cut.

"Won't let what take me?"

"The lies you tell yourself to cope with the pain and your fear. I love you. You're going to stay here with me. You're not going to hurt like this forever."

"Maraye, I love you. I'm sorry. I'm sorry I'm so weak."

"We can be weak together, Emmett."

`"Maraye?"

"Yes?"

"I really do love you."

She wipes my face with her sleeve and I wipe hers.

"Don't ever do that again. I mean it. I'll never forgive you." As she finishes speaking, she squeezes the side of my head firmly and stares into me.

"I won't, Maraye. I'll be okay. I'm not irreparably broken. I can't be … I have so much left to give of myself. I have to believe I haven't given it all … not yet."

"I mean it, Emmett. If you're going to do that again, just leave me now. I won't be with you. I'll never forgive you if you do this again."

She stares at for a few moments and releases me. I'm beginning to shake uncontrollably from my wet clothing and the cold wind. I can practically feel my joints rattling together.

"Maraye, will you come be warm with me?"

"I'd like that a lot," she says.

CHAPTER 11

Charlie rests with me on the cabin porch. He whines next to me. "How ya doing, Charlie?" I ask rhetorically.

Fog lifts off the lake. I stare out at it as I rest my arms on the porch-railing think about what I'm going to do now. I look down when Charlie brushes my leg.

"We're going to be alright, aren't we?" I ask as I kneel to run my fingers through his brown coat. "Come on boy."

We walk down to the marina. Charlie runs beside me. He knows what's coming next as I lift him into the boat and push off the dock. The scene around me fills me up and I feel incredibly human. I see myself as a beautiful, unstable mess of a human. A blood red moon shines down on us. The world feels warmer.

When I reach the middle of the lake I lay back and stare into the sky. Charlie rests his head on my stomach. There's no light anywhere, just the moon and stars. I'm happy to call this place my home but I miss Maraye. Charlie's head jerks up and he barks, almost as if he's welcoming me back to life.

"We're gonna be just fine," I whisper to him.

The air is a warm kind of moist. It feels good on my skin. I smell honeysuckle drifting across the water. It's been a long war and I feel like the burnt out soldier who made it home alive. Something's been lifted off of me. The spruce forest rests silently on either side of me. I realize that the guilt that's relentlessly hounded me is growing quieter and silencing itself.

I've begun to study independently, picking up books and essays on physics and literature. It's nice to feel my desire for education returning. In the morning I jog on the shoreline of the lake and through some trails in the forest. I'm becoming disciplined once again, even going so far as to cut and comb my hair

Before I sleep I normally lie awake and think of the future. I've resolved that I can't understand life the way I can understand an equation or a formula. For so long I've wanted to find concrete answers or die trying. It's hard at first to find comfort in not knowing or to make peace with it. But I think it's the only way to make it in this life. Getting stuck on a question only makes me estranged from the world.

I almost always smile now when I think of Lenai. I pity those who die without love, or worse, those who never know it. I consider myself fortunate to have known it and to have known it so well. I consider myself fortunate to know it now. The time has come for me to be born again. If I'm going to continue living, I'm resigned to do it well.

And so on a Wednesday morning I take a seat in the wooden swing on the porch. I reach into my pocket and pull my phone from it. Sonya sounds tired when she answers my call.

"Hello?" her tired voice blares through my speaker so I pull it away.

"Sonya?"

"Emmett? How are you? Is everything okay?" She sounds worried and I imagine her quickly sitting up in fear.

"Yes, everything's fine. Are you alright?"

"I'm good. I'm glad to hear from you. You sound good," she says.

"I am good. I'm much better," I tell her. "Listen there's something I need to tell you." I try not to sound nervous but I can feel the perspiration accumulating and I struggle to speak clearly.

"Okay," she says. "What is it?"

"I'm in love ..."

"Oh Emmett, is it Maraye?"

"Yes," I say. "Sonya ... I love Lenai very much."

"I know," she responds. "You never need to feel guilty, Emmett. I want you to be happy and so would Lenai."

"I still need you to be a part of my life," I tell her.

"I will always be here for you Emmett. I am so very happy for you."

"Sonya?"

"Yes, Emmett?"

"I'm going to be better, alright?"

"I know you are. I'm very proud of you."

On Thursday I wake to see Maraye. I watch her through my bedroom window. She's sitting in the bed of poppies looking out at the water. Slowly and decisively I pull on some clothes, comb my hair and walk out to her. She's silent as I sit next to her.

"I missed you." I tell her. "How was California?"

"It was hot but I liked it." She replies.

"And your dad?"

"It was a nice visit. I'm glad you made me go. We're going to call each other more often."

"Good," I say.

"It's beautiful, isn't it?" she asks me, looking out at the trees.

"It really is ..." I say thoughtfully.

"There's so much beauty, so much memory in this one little patch, isn't there?"

"Yes ..." I say, thinking of our talks on the porch, of Jack and Charlie.

She smiles at me and rises to her feet. "Come on, let's go walk."

"Walk where?" I ask.

"Into our forest," she says smiling.

My odyssey continues as we walk into the shadow of the forest. This is our home now. This is where my odyssey has taken me. I've had to endure and triumph and suffer and fall to rise again. I've had to love and break only to love and break once more. It's all I've got, this love thing. It's all I have to counter the insipid forces of despair and hatred and weakness. And it's enough to overcome those things. It's enough to overcome death itself.

"Maraye, how do you feel about aimlessly wandering the earth with me for a while?"

"Really?" she asks.

"Yeah," I say. "I mean, eventually we'll have to do something productive but there's a big world out there. Let's go see it together. I need to rebuild my sense of awe."

"Are you sure you're ready for that? You're ready to move on with me?" she asks, taking my hand in hers.

"Yes," I say. "It's time to let go. It's time to love again. I've decided that's what people need to keep on living even when life doesn't make sense. We need to love, even if it's just one person. Even if we love poorly."

And we are just together. The two of us. This is how life goes on, driven ever forward by love.

How To Support Shane Crash

At Civitas Press, we believe in the power of social networking to help get the word out. As a reader of this book, we appreciate your voice in helping Shane spread the word about his work. If you would like to support Shane and help promote this book, please consider the following options:

- Recommend this book to those in your social network, community, work or class;

- Review the book on Amazon;

- Share a link to the book on Facebook or Twitter;

- Give the book to a friend who could help spread the word;

- Email those in your personal or professional network with information about the book and a link to Amazon;

- Blog about the book and provide a link to Amazon;

- Recommend the book to your book club.

Please feel free to contact Shane for interviews, media relations, guest blog posts, and speaking engagements. You can contact him at: shanenomads@yahoo.com

www.ingramcontent.com/pod-product-compliance
Lightning Source LLC
Chambersburg PA
CBHW070526260626
47161CB00004B/1639